DURANGO

Gary Hart

FULCRUM
GOLDEN, COLORADO

749
8-12 $15.95

© 2012 by Gary Hart

PUBLISHER'S NOTE: This is a work of fiction. Names, characters, places, and incidents either are the product of the author's imagination or are used fictitiously.

Library of Congress Cataloging-in-Publication Data
Hart, Gary, 1936-
  Durango / Gary Hart.
    p. cm.
  ISBN 978-1-55591-670-1 (pbk.)
  1. Durango (Colo.)--Fiction. 2. Political fiction. I. Title.
  PS3558.A6776D87 2012
  813'.54--dc23
                                2011047865

Printed in the United States of America
0 9 8 7 6 5 4 3 2 1

Design by Jack Lenzo

Fulcrum Publishing
4690 Table Mountain Dr., Ste. 100
Golden, CO 80403
800-992-2908 • 303-277-1623
www.fulcrumbooks.com

For the good people of Durango
and Ignacio

All this must come to pass. A soothsayer,

And a Trojan soothsayer at that, has foretold it.

This is the summer of the fall of Troy.

It'll be talked about for ever and you're to be

The hero that was healed and then went on

To heal the wound of the Trojan war itself.

—Seamus Heaney, *The Cure at Troy*:
A Version of Sophocles' Philoctetes

PART ONE

1.

Rescuing lost things would be easier if God would cooperate. Every time somebody's cow or calf, or both, or some dumb flatlander got themselves stranded up there in the high country, it seems that there's a storm of some kind.

Now here was Harv saying, Say, Dan, I know it looks kind of bad out there. But I got a good old cow and a spring calf up above there. He had paused and coughed apologetically. I was wonderin' if you could give me a hand bringin' 'em down.

Sheridan had figured what it was when the phone rang. Every spring, Harv let his cows go up too high too soon and then, just about this time every spring, one or two got lost or stranded. And every spring the call came. Same words. Same cough.

But hell, he thought, pulling on the boots that had even more creases than his face, Harv was a good decade older than he was, and he wasn't getting around too well. Besides, situation reversed, Harv would do the same for him. But Harv had never had to and, he thought wryly, never would have to. The few cattle he did run would never be allowed to graze up high this early in the cantankerous spring storm season.

He pulled on the flannel-lined denim jacket, turned up the wool collar, and pulled on his worn-out work gloves. He told Toby, his border collie, he'd be back. Outdoors he bent against the rising wind to get to the barn. Glancing to the northwest, he guessed fifteen minutes for the snow. Depending where the cow had got herself and her calf to, it would take the better part of an hour to find them and most of another hour to bring them down.

He hefted the saddle, soft from a recent oiling, down from its mounting, and the horse, noisily munching his supper oats, gave him the sad eye. *Not tonight*, the look said. *Not while I'm having my supper.* Sheridan patted the solid rump and said, The oats'll be here when we get back. For himself, he was glad he had remembered to get a fresh bottle of Jameson. He led the horse out of the barn, swung up, and the horse shook his head vigorously as he felt the heel tap.

Sheridan said, Okay Red, let's go.

Harvey Waldron had been a neighbor, had been his father's neighbor, so long he couldn't remember since when. A hogback ridge separated their properties up the tail end of the old Florida Road. Harv tried to run thirty or forty head of Herefords all by himself long after he should. Dan, he'd say, what else I got to do? Just me and the cows, he'd say. I figure, he'd always say, when the cows go, I go.

That being the situation, what else could he do than help Harv bring down a cow or two every spring?

He made good time in the dimming light, going up the diminishing dirt road that tailed off into a trail in the draw leading to the upper reaches of his property. He knew Harv would meet him where his horse trail met a similar one rising above the Waldron meadow to the east. Now the snow came. And with it, the wind. And it didn't start slowly. It arrived full force. The electricity along Florida Road was down, yet again, and the forecast from his hand-cranked radio had predicted a foot or more of snow. He saw Harv sitting his horse just ahead in the driving snow and knew they had to find the cow and calf right quickly.

Thanks, Dan, Harv muttered through his thick mustache. I'll do the same for you one of these days. Then he chuckled, Except I know I won't have to.

Doesn't matter, Harv, Sheridan shouted back as he moved his horse out in front and followed the trail higher. It's the thought that counts, he shouted over the wind. Where do you reckon this cow of yours is?

Where they always go, Dan, Harv shouted, up in those aspen trees at the top end of my place. Maybe even over into the federal land.

Sheridan heel-tapped his big red horse and climbed more quickly. The high aspen grove was another thirty minutes at least. They climbed in silence, the horses and men blowing serious clouds of steam. Loose rocks clattered under shod hooves. He could see no more than thirty feet, probably less, ahead. The horse snorted and shook his head, thinking of oats. If a horse had a memory and could count—and for all Sheridan knew, this horse could—he would know it would be an hour or more before he got back to his oats and the barn's shelter.

Considerable time passed as the climb continued, the stiff wind blowing snow sideways from the northwest. They emerged into a small, high meadow, and he thought he could see the aspen grove a football field away. Harv shouted, She's up there. He knew Harv couldn't see that far, particularly in a spring blizzard, so he listened. Sure enough, there was a faint, far-off, buffered bellow. He suddenly remembered he hadn't holstered his rifle and hoped to God a cat hadn't gotten after the calf.

They followed the intermittent bellowing as it became less muffled. Fifty yards, then twenty-five. His horse snorted again and he knew, from certain experience, that if a cat had gotten there first, the horse wouldn't go much farther. He cursed again about the forgotten Winchester. Harv could afford to lose a calf a lot easier than he could afford to lose a horse that had taken a dozen years to become an extension of his own body.

He swung down from the horse and, grunting, Harv followed. Both carried lariat rope. Eyes wide and terror-stricken, the cow stomped and thrashed around in the thick aspen growth. The month-old calf stood still, threatened with trampling by the mother cow. Sheridan got within a dozen feet of the frantic cow and easily tossed the lariat rope over her head, and it settled around her neck. He looped the rope around the saddle pommel as Harv lassoed the calf and did likewise.

The cow now calmed and let the horse lead her out of the grove. The calf seemed satisfied to follow. Now, he thought, the hard part begins. Harv, he shouted through the wind's howl, you start down there with your calf and I'll bring the old lady down right behind you. Harv nodded and mounted up. Sheridan hoped to hell Harv wouldn't get lost going down, but he trusted him to know the trails— even those now drifting heavily with snow—on his own property deeded to the Waldrons by some Indian chief well over a century before.

Visibility was now almost totally gone. He let the reins loose on the tall horse, knowing that oats were as good a horse-compass as anything. Harv's mustache was hoary-thick with a mixture of frozen tobacco juice and snow. His own eyebrows, he imagined, looked much the same—minus the tobacco juice. The snow drove sideways at about thirty miles an hour. He brushed snow away from his horse's eyes as the sure-footed creature methodically plowed through the drifts now up to his knees. Sheridan pulled the aged Stetson lower over his forehead.

They got to the fork connecting the horse trails from the two properties, and he followed Harv down toward his outbuildings, now a quarter of a mile ahead. Harv shouted back to him, Give me that lead rope and I'll take her on in. Sheridan shook his head *no*. If the cow got spooked or rambunctious, Harv could well be tossed from his horse and end up frozen. He waved him forward. After another ten minutes or so, they got to the cow pasture. They both dismounted, untied their bovine wards, and turned them into the fenced pasture with their closely huddled herd. The cow lowed and bellowed, and the calf trotted to join her in the dense mass.

Come on in for a drink, Harv shouted over the wind. You've earned it.

He shook his head and shouted back, Next time. You'll owe me one.

I owe you a helluva lot more than one, Harv shouted back and waved his arm toward the house.

Sheridan shook his head again and swung up into the tall saddle. He touched his hat, now thick with snow, and reined his horse around. They went back up the Waldron trail to the fork and made a U-turn down toward his own place. Another ten or fifteen minutes later, he dismounted and led the horse back into his stable barn. He lifted off the heavy saddle and blanket, hung them on their hooks, and proceeded to knock the caked snow from the horse's hide. He led the big creature over to his stall and let him start on the oats as he wiped him down with a heavy horse towel. He then brushed him vigorously, as much to stimulate circulation as to groom, and finally toweled him off again.

The animal stomped a foot now and then, as if to say, *You've done your job. Now let me enjoy these oats. I think I've earned them.*

Sheridan smacked the horse's rump by way of thanks and compliment and then headed out through the blizzard to his own smoldering fireplace and the Jameson.

2.

Well, here he comes, Sam Maynard observed. Sam always sat at their corner table by the café window in the seat that gave him the best view of the street and anyone coming up the sidewalk. Let's act like we don't know about his adventure, he muttered.

The Monday, and sometimes Friday, coffee club had become a fixture. Mr. Murphy had started it, and Sam had been an original attendee. The professor scheduled his history classes at Fort Lewis College so that Monday and Friday mornings around eight were free. Bill Van Ness, the high school principal, discovered the conclave and managed to happen by once or twice a week. And from time to time, Dan Sheridan found himself in the neighborhood of the café on Durango's Main Avenue, with the mural of Jack Dempsey on the outside wall that dated to sometime around the turn of the century—the twentieth, that is.

Sheridan came through the door, hung his hat on the coat tree, and took the last seat at the table. He nodded all around.

You get much snow up your way? Mr. Murphy asked.

A good bit, Sheridan said. Happens every year around this time.

The men sipped their coffee and gave this some thought. The professor said, Kind of makes you wonder about climate changing. Big snow like that. Even so, he continued, all the material I've read convinces me it's the real deal. Something we have to deal with.

Suppose so, Sheridan allowed, cutting off what could have been a disquisition on climate.

Sam grinned and said, Your cattle okay? The others stared at him. They had known he couldn't resist this.

Yep, Sheridan said.

How's old Harv doing? Sam persisted after a brief silence. The others stared harder. They wanted to see if Sheridan would discuss the adventure on his own.

Harv's doin' fine, he said, so far as I would know. Now they knew he wasn't going to volunteer anything.

Well, Sam said, there's some talk going around about you and Harv and some cows. The professor studied the smoked-stained ceiling.

Over the top of his steamy cup, Sheridan looked at Sam. Harv did have a cow and calf up at the top of his place when the snow came in, he allowed. We went up and got 'em and brought 'em down. That's pretty much it.

The regulars considered this. Pretty bad snow Friday evening, Bill Van Ness said.

Sheridan said, Hmmm.

Harv's telling folks you saved his cow and calf, Sam said.

I wouldn't know about that, Sheridan said, reaching for the coffeepot. Harv's been known to have a good imagination.

Soon the conversation wandered off to the Durango High School's chances at the state basketball tournament, whether the tourists would show up and when, and a number of other topics of the day. It was a standing, though unspoken, rule that politics would rarely be discussed.

The Sheridan family went back three generations in Durango. The grandfather was buried on the property, as was his son. It was generally assumed the grandson would someday join them in the small fenced plot in a corner of the high meadow beyond the top of Florida Road. Some said the original Sheridan somehow traced back to the Civil War general Little Phil. Even though the County Cavan roots were there and the dates worked out, more or less, the old man had steadfastly denied it, as much as anything else because Philip Sheridan had treated the western Indians brutally following the war.

Daniel Sheridan made no claim one way or the other.

Though well enough known in the community, Sheridan kept to himself, as they said, and his life was singular if not solitary. He was known to visit the local cinema on occasion when a movie worth seeing came to town. That itself was rare enough. And even more rarely he would be seen at the Strater Hotel dining room at a back corner table, on almost every one of those occasions in the company of a tall, dark-haired woman. She was also known in town, though her habits were at least as closely guarded as Sheridan's.

Caroline Chandler's place was about ten or twelve miles northwest of town, around where Quinn Creek met Johnson Creek. Her acreage was smaller than Sheridan's, and she had no time for cattle. What she had time for, aside from the rare dinners with Sheridan, was a matter of some mystery. But Durango was not a town given to prying into the lives of its citizens, especially those with deep and lasting roots. The town observed an almost nineteenth-century concern for privacy and respect for personal idiosyncrasy.

Well, then, Mr. Murphy said, that's our excitement for the week. Rescued cow and calf. Doesn't take much around here.

The professor, more attuned to Sheridan's moods than the others, happily announced that enrollment at Fort Lewis College was going to be up for the next fall. Well, that's good, they all agreed. The kids bought stuff in town, frequented the bars and restaurants, and, compared to their generation elsewhere, generally behaved well. The college was a definite boost to the local economy.

Sheridan pushed back from the table, fetched his hat, and nodded all around. See you Friday, Sam said, more by way of a question. Sheridan waved over his shoulder.

Now Harv said it was a real tough trick to bring that cow and calf down, Mr. Murphy said. Dan wasn't about to admit it.

Bill Van Ness said, You didn't expect him to, did you?

Not especially, Mr. Murphy replied.

Sam inquired cautiously, Do you think he'll ever be back to his old self...the way he was?

The table was silent. I wouldn't hold my breath, Mr. Murphy finally said. If he's not his old self by now, he probably won't ever be…and even so, Ms. Chandler would be the one to know. He nodded across the street to where she was parking her car.

3.

In 1868, the federal government entered into a treaty with the consolidated bands of Ute people. Within a few decades, federal policies and the pressures of western expansion would divide the Ute people into three distinct tribes, one of which is the Southern Ute Tribe. By the late twentieth century, the tribe was down to fewer than 1,500 members, though well before the Spanish came, their ancestors had migrated around and across most of what became Colorado and large parts of New Mexico and Utah. In the late nineteenth century, the Ute Strip, basically desert land roughly fifteen miles wide and seventy-five miles long, was created by the government and became the permanent Southern Ute reservation. By the mid-1930s, even that rough terrain near the corner of Colorado, Utah, and New Mexico was half-owned by non-Indians. And the whites had managed to get much of the prime land near the several rivers and streams crossing the Southern Ute reservation.

Like everywhere else in the arid and semiarid West, there was little that could be done with the land unless you had water. A few cows might be grazed on the scrub brush and clumps of weeds, but there would be no crops for sale or gardens for family food without water. And the water did not ordinarily come from rainfall. It resulted from the high

mountain snows and it had to be stored when the spring
runoff from the San Juan Mountain range, just north and
east of the reservation, came. The Animas and La Plata rivers, as well as the Florida and lesser streams, transited the
reservation. But the tribe had no storage facilities for irrigation or domestic use. If you did not have property along
one of those streams, and the means to divert it, you were
living a life dominated by wind and dust, and little else.

Up until the 1960s, the Southern Utes, with few
exceptions, lived pretty much hand to mouth. The small
tribal treasury provided no more than one or two hundred
dollars a year per tribal member. And by and large, members of the tribe were at the end of the employment chain
in and around town.

By the 1960s, however, things began to change. Tourism in the spectacularly beautiful region, with its national
forests and then wilderness areas, jagged peaks, ancient
Native American ruins, wild streams, partially restored
mining towns, nature and horse-riding trails, and plenti-
ful campgrounds, brought a wave of economic growth.
Increasing numbers of city dwellers, confronting urban
crowding and pollution, visited the region, went back home
and sold out, and moved to the area permanently. But all
this activity and all these new people needed more of what
was already lacking: water.

Not too long thereafter, a vast national search for
energy resources began. As early as the 1950s, areas around
Durango were mined for a new vital resource—uranium—
first for nuclear weapons and then for nuclear power plants.
But there was also coal, and there was oil and natural gas.

The confluence of tourism, urban escapees, and energy

development meant that water from the San Juan snows could not continue to run off down the streambeds to New Mexico and Arizona. It had to be stored. And the only way to store it was to build dams, more particularly a dam collecting water from the Animas and La Plata rivers.

The federal government, in the form of the Department of the Interior's Bureau of Reclamation, was only too glad to help. It was beginning to run out of places to build dams in the West. But as planning began for the Animas–La Plata Dam around 1968, resistance arose. All those people who had recently moved into the area, now having put their roots down, were less than enthusiastic about increasing the water supply that would then encourage their former neighbors back East to come out and join them, thus bringing the congestion they themselves had only recently and eagerly escaped. The newcomers soon joined old-timers who already thought Durango over-crowded to organize opposition to the dam. Both newcomers and old-timers found support from traditional conservation and newer environmental groups opposed to dams virtually anywhere. By the late 1970s they found a political champion in Jimmy Carter.

The town of Durango itself had begun to emerge in 1880 when an entrepreneur named William Jackson Palmer brought the Denver & Rio Grande Railroad all the way to southwestern Colorado. He played a central role in laying out the very grid that would become the town, surveying and selling lots, and he saw to it that there were people out there on his railroad line who would take his trains back and forth to Silverton and Denver, miners who would come to work at the smelter built there a few years after, goods that would fill his outbound boxcars, and cattle that would crowd the inbound cattle cars back to Denver.

Over the years a frontier mystique grew up around Durango as embodying an ideal western small-town-America style of living that was human scale. People knew each other. They attended their various churches with those they worked with during the week. Parents knew teachers. Shopkeepers knew customers. Insurance agents, auto dealers, repair shops, bankers, lawyers, and cowboys mixed and mingled. It was an honest place. It was solid and trustworthy. It was about as close to perfect as a place could get.

Who wanted mining trucks, oil rigs, gypsy roughnecks breaking up Saturday night bars, bigger, noisier hotels, big chain stores, and eventually, inevitably, back-office service representatives in Bangladesh handling your insurance claims? Stop development. Stop the dam. So, peaceful Durango, representing western America if not all America in the second half of the twentieth century, found itself deeply divided.

There was one more element in this equation, however, that came into play. The Southern Ute Tribe had historic claims to water rights on the Animas and the La Plata. If any dams were built upstream for the Durango city folk, a proportionate share had to go to the Utes. And finally, after decades of hanging on in at best marginal conditions, the Utes saw the dam as offering the possibility of a major step up.

Now the equation was complicated. The pro-dam development faction had the Indian tribes on its side. And the anti-dam, anti-development faction—who by nature would normally have found themselves on the side of the hapless, downtrodden, neglected, and cheated Native Americans—found themselves opposing a substantial means for Ute improvement and self-advancement.

Out of a mixture of water and minerals emerged a serpent of greed that threatened to poison this idyllic community.

4.

Sheridan made room at his drugstore table for Caroline Chandler. You've already had plenty of caffeine with the boys, she said.

A little, he said. But on a Monday morning there's always need for more.

Without being asked, the waitress brought two large mugs of very strong coffee. Her raised eyebrows asked, Anything else? They both shook their heads.

Had my annual spring roundup with Harv Waldron, he said presently. I'm gettin' too old for this. It's my good deed for the week.

Oh, Daniel, she said, patting his rough hand, you'll be bringing Harv's cows down decades from now.

Hope to God not, he said. Though the only good part was that the excursion in the blizzard gave me an excuse for an extra Jameson.

It *is* good sleep medicine, she said with a tone of experience.

How're things up at your place? he asked.

No complaints, she said. I think I owe you a dinner.

He chuckled. That's usually a signal that you've got a

big rock that needs moving or a board loose somewhere.

She looked offended. Now, that's cruel. I've fed you plenty of times where you haven't had to work for it.

He looked at her through lowered eyebrows and presented a tight smile. Not sure how you mean that.

She laughed. You know how I mean it. Don't be cute. I could put you to work for six months around my place patching and fixing, but I'd have to feed you the whole time, and I can't afford it.

Will work for food, he said. Maybe a little kindness from time to time wouldn't hurt, either.

Let's not go there, she smiled. I know your definition of "kindness."

Just a healthy boy, he said, who gets lonely from time to time.

They both tried the cooling coffee, each ransacking memory for the long history of a complicated friendship. This cabinet of memories had hidden compartments of happiness and drawers of various sizes stuffed with webs of conflict and controversy. An air of irresolution pervaded every corner.

She broke the reverie. Been down to see Leonard Cloud recently?

The deep crease between his eyebrows deepened. We keep in touch. After a moment, he said, Why bring that up?

You know I can't leave it totally alone, she said. It's your life. And it's my life as well. Then after a pause she added, It's not over, you know.

Well, it sure as hell is for me, he grunted, and signaled for more coffee.

We're not going to pursue it, she said, at least not here,

not now. But you know how I feel. A time will come when it has to come out. And it will. It has to, Daniel. Otherwise, there's no justice in this world.

He snorted. No justice. I'd say the no justice side wins this one.

After the coffee was refilled, he said, The Utes are doing well and that's all I care about. Talk about justice. They had to wait over a hundred years. But they're finally getting what they deserve. Leonard says the royalties are rolling in.

What I've heard, she said.

He's so smart, Sheridan continued. He's got the tribal council to create a trust fund. Sam's law firm helped 'em set it up. Most of the royalty money goes there. And they've got a plan to put that into education for several generations of tribal kids. They'll still have plenty left over for really decent housing for the families. And they've started work on the senior center and a new community center in Ignacio.

She said, They've finally got a chance to live like real ordinary human beings. She wanted to say more, to tell him that she had advised the Ute tribal council on how to set up a durable trust fund, but she decided it could wait until later.

He leaned back in his chair. Even poor, they were the most ordinary human beings I ever met. It's kinda interesting to wonder whether they'd get back on their horses and roam again if they could.

Be a little hard, she said, dragging their stuff across interstates and through a bunch of parking lots and truck stops.

He laughed. Sure enough. Wouldn't be the same as the old days, now would it? I just hope they don't go to hell with most of the rest of modern civilization. There'll be a few of them that'll pack up and buy some big old houses in Hollywood. He shook his head.

Have you gone to hell, Daniel? she asked.

He laughed again. Course not. If I had, you wouldn't be here, would you? And besides, I'm not big rich, in case you hadn't noticed.

That's a good question, she said. I suppose I would be here. I'd keep trying to save your soul.

Well, I appreciate that, Miss Missionary, he chuckled. My soul sure does want savin'.

If I cook something Friday, will you tell me more about what the tribe's doing? she asked. It's the only way I can find out.

Well, he said, you know Leonard as well as I do. Just get on your horse and ride out there. He'd love to see you. After a pause he said, But you know me well enough to know I'm not going to turn down a supper.

They rose, he threw a bill on the table, and they headed for the door. I'll bring the Jameson, he said as he touched her shoulder, then raised a hand in parting.

5.

He didn't tell Caroline about the ceremony. He rarely did.

The day after his adventure with Harv Waldron's cows, he had indeed met with Leonard Cloud, the tribal chairman. Then he had gone to the weathered house owned by the Southern Ute's venerable holy man on the outskirts of Ignacio. Two Hawks was well into his eighties. No one, including himself, was quite sure of the year of his birth in the early twentieth century. From his earliest years, Two Hawks had seen spirits in the wind and water. He prayed to the four compass points and the four seasons. And he communed with all the creatures. Each species of tree— sage, juniper, pinion—had its own spirit, and all required respect and reverence. The birds were messengers on the wing. Though he was an occasional meat-eater, there was no memory in the tribe of him ever purposefully harming a living thing. A rattler deserved his own space. Two Hawks would step well around.

One of Sheridan's earliest memories was of his father taking him to meet Two Hawks, then a vigorous man in his mid-thirties. He was tall and lean, even then with lined cheeks and narrow hips. The young Sheridan watched with keen eyes as the two men conversed. They spoke in short sentences punctuated by long silences. Their mood was inevitably solemn. Most often, Sheridan's father asked questions and listened quietly as Two Hawks responded.

They talked about ordinary things—weather, water, people, and sometimes current events in the outside world. Occasionally, however, Sheridan observed periods of meditation and quiet communication, almost a kind of worship. Throughout his growing-up years, he went with his father on these sojourns two or three times a year, and he lent himself more easily to the temper and found in the silences—even more than in the conversation—a form of communion. By the time he was an adult and after his father's passing, he assumed this pattern. And he watched Two Hawks grow older, even thinner, and become increasingly a part of all things, animate and inanimate, around him. It seemed that the older the Ute became, the more he merged into his natural environment and became a part of the scrub trees, cactus, birds, wildflowers, and sage that were part of his nature.

A few years before, in the time of the trouble, Sheridan had sought the companionship and wisdom of the aging holy man. Two Hawks had helped save his sanity and possibly even his soul.

Now, the day after the storm, Sheridan parked outside Two Hawks's old house. He waited and watched, as always, patient so as not to intrude on the holy man's space. Before long, he saw the thin arm in the doorway beckoning him inside.

The Ute made tea using local herbs. They sat for a period and thought.

Sheridan said, Did the snow get down this far?

Two Hawks nodded. Some. Not as much as you, though.

Sheridan related the lost cow incident from the previous Friday night.

The mother cow risked her calf's life to see if you really cared about them, Two Hawks said and then chuckled.

She could've found a better way to settle that question, Sheridan said. How are things here? he asked, meaning the reservation.

I am told we are now wealthy people, Two Hawks said. The chairman has done a good job keeping our faith. We are nature's people, not the people of your things. He said "things" in such a way that Sheridan knew he meant cars, appliances, and trinkets.

But all this money will change us...for good and for bad. Our young people will have better learning. Then they will leave this place. We will have better houses. He surveyed his own primitive surroundings. But we will burn more coal to heat and light. We'll have bigger pickups. They will burn more fuel. Humans are the last creatures to learn about the balance in nature. Two Hawks held both hands palms up as if measuring weights on a scale. Every use has a price, he continued. Usually the price is greater than the use we seek. The less necessary the use, the greater the waste.

Will there still be Utes in fifty, a hundred years? Sheridan asked.

Come ask me then, Two Hawks smiled. I will be a juniper down near the Animas…if the Spirit thinks I am worthy.

Sheridan smiled also. Why not a cougar?

Oh, I have not earned a cougar spirit yet. It will take time. Much more than the years I have had. The cougar spirit is very big. He is the chief of these parts. It is a very big spirit. It must be earned.

How do you earn that spirit? Sheridan asked.

Two Hawks looked through the doorway, his stare a hundred miles downrange. Strength. Patience. Courage. Fortitude…a good word. Wisdom. Mostly wisdom.

You seem pretty wise to me, Sheridan offered.

If you were not my good friend, Two Hawks said, I would say that your people's idea of wisdom is pretty thin. Wisdom needs time and patience. It needs thinking. It needs praying. It is a gift, but you must earn this gift.

His voice was reedy and thin, but forceful. His arrow-straight back had begun to bow at the shoulders. His ancient shirt hung on his frame as on a scarecrow. Dust briefly blew past the open doorway. They were silent for a time. Sheridan knew the holy man had something to say.

Two Hawks hummed a chant quietly, as if in a kind of trance. Then he said, The first time it was water. Long ago. When I was a boy, our ancient holy men, older even than I am now, said that the holy men for generations before them, before memory, said the second time would be fire.

Sheridan inhaled and waited.

Fire. Very big fire.

Like a forest fire? Sheridan asked.

Much bigger. Intense fire. Bigger than a mountain blowing up. Man-made. As hot as the sun.

Well, Sheridan said, that has to be something nuclear. He waited and said, Is that it?

Two Hawks shook his head. I don't know. I am told that the nuclear things burn as hot as the sun. I don't know anything else man has created that does. If it burns, it will destroy the whole earth. It will be a judgment. The Spirit will decide things have gone too far. We cannot act as if we were gods. We cannot hold such power.

The government says we're trying to get rid of some of this stuff. The bombs, Sheridan said.

All. It all must be destroyed. Or it will be used. The ancient people said the fire could not be contained if it started. That's all I know.

Two Hawks presently held up a hand. Sheridan had become familiar with this sign. He waited and watched, breathing quietly and looking into the distance. The ancient Ute hummed in rhythm and closed his eyes. After a moment he began a prayer, a prayer for all the creatures, great and small, for the winged things, for the creepy-crawly creatures, for the trees and flowers, for water and wind, for all things in nature. Then he prayed for the people, his own

Ute people and people in Durango and wherever there were people. He asked the Spirit's blessing on all things.

Sheridan breathed softly. He knew the rest to come.

Two Hawks asked the Spirit to heal his friend Sheridan. He reminded the Spirit that Sheridan was a worthy man, an honest man. Sheridan and his father and his father's father had been friends to the Utes. Sheridan had earned the Spirit's blessing. Sheridan needed the Spirit's blessing. Then he became silent.

His heart heavy, Sheridan waited in silence. Though burdened by his own history, as always he felt better for the prayer and the blessing. Then both men stood. Two Hawks walked him to the open door. They did not shake hands in the fashion of civilization. But when Sheridan reached his pickup, he turned and held up his hand by way of thanks.

Visions of the fire to end all life had been in the back of Sheridan's mind ever since.

6.

Madam Chairwoman, Sheridan said, we're going to have to resolve the Animas–La Plata issue one of these days. This commission has gone back and forth, up and down, and sooner or later the state and the feds are going to want our judgment on the matter.

Recently elected to the commission at this point years ago, Sheridan would later become its chair.

Mr. Sheridan, said Dolores Raymond, chairwoman of the La Plata County Commission, you know well enough that there are five of us here, and two of us are for it, two of us are against it, and one of us—she looked down the horseshoe-curved table to her right—can't make up his mind.

Well, Sheridan said, our members of Congress have to vote on the funds for the project in next year's budget, and I don't know about you, but they are pestering me for a decision.

Me too, Dolores Raymond said. What's your opinion these days, Mr. Ralph?

The young man on the right end of the table said, Well, as the newest member of the County Commission—he scratched his head—it's still pretty confusing to me. Half the people in my district want it and half don't want it.

Welcome to elective office, Sheridan said.

All but the youngish man smiled, and the reporter for the *Durango Herald* made a note.

The thing is, Ralph said, it does get down to growth or no-growth. I can see how the water helps the energy people and the developers. But like Mrs. Raymond here, I can see, even as a newcomer to this area, how too much, too soon will mess this place up. Like a lot of new people, I came here because Durango and this county are a good place to live and to raise children just the way they are.

Lots of dollars to be made, Mr. Ralph, Sheridan said, by lots of people in the dollar-making business.

Well, you're for the project, Ralph said, and you've lived here forever. How come you're for it?

Sheridan looked at the ceiling with a wry smile, Not quite forever, Mr. Ralph. I'm not Methuselah. Just Methuselah's son. But to answer your question, it's the Utes. Half the people I represent want this project and half don't want it, just like you, but the final straw for me was the Southern Utes getting the water they need to carry out their energy development program, Red Willow, and improve the lives of their people. Simple matter of justice.

In the back of the meeting room, packed with two hundred or so people, sat two men, one about Commissioner Ralph's age, the other a well-turned-out man in his late fifties. Both wore expensive suits and stood out from the everyday La Plata County crowd around them. The younger man took detailed notes. Occasionally they whispered to each other.

The floor was opened for public comment and, as usual, a number of citizens queued at the microphones. As at many commission meetings in the years before, individual comments were about equally divided between those who didn't understand why the "government" didn't just get on with it and build the dam and those who decried the damage to the environment and the quality of life around Durango. Sheridan and the other commissioners listened attentively and sometimes nodded in agreement or disagreement. Once or twice the commissioners asked questions of the more informed citizens or chastised those who chose an extremist stance, one way or the other.

———————

That all occurred some twelve years before. But that evening, and many like it in the monthly county commission cycle, had often crossed Sheridan's mind in the years since. He remembered noting the two well-dressed men, strangers to him, and wondering what had brought them there. Very soon thereafter he was to find out.

In the meantime, the prolonged, troublesome, and divisive Animas–La Plata Dam project had waxed and waned over years and then decades, surviving largely on annual congressional appropriations for "study" funds to keep the project alive another year in the hope that divine intervention or rare human wisdom might resolve it one way or the other.

For the minority of those in the Durango community who did not worry about the project or who tried to find a balance between growth and preservation, the feeling was that a dam of some dimensions would ultimately be built, if for no other reason than because of what came to be shorthanded as the "Sheridan position": the Southern Utes deserved and needed their fair share of the water stored above the dam. There was some degree of white guilt in this. But the Utes had built up a store of moral capital over many decades, and the issue of justice was a powerful one.

Sheridan often used that word—*justice*—when he could not think of a better one. For him it meant what was right. Though he had a year or so of law school, he did not philosophize about it. And he did not use it to preach. But he did remember a line he had seen on a rare trip to Washington. It was on the wall in the Jefferson Memorial rotunda. "I tremble for my country when I reflect that God is just." Jefferson's conscience had plagued him about slavery. Sheridan had a similar sense about the Utes.

A few days after that county commission meeting, Sheridan had gotten a call from the younger of the two men who had been at the back of the meeting hall. He called himself Matthew Palmer—just call me Matt—and said that he and his boss, Mr. Stone, would appreciate the

pleasure of lunch with Mr. Sheridan. What might this be
about? Sheridan had asked. He tried not to sound too wary.
Matt Palmer had responded that they wished to discuss
the Animas–La Plata project. They certainly shared Mr.
Sheridan's concern for the Southern Ute Tribe. They represented a company that wished to help the Utes develop
their mineral resources as a means of providing a better life
for people too long left out of modern advancement.

On that occasion, Sheridan had chosen not to test the
young Palmer's bona fides. But he did, at least in his mind,
do what his father had long ago taught him: When you
hear some notion that seems too good to be true, put your
hand on your wallet.

With a measure of native caution, Sheridan joined the
two men at the Strater Hotel dining room for lunch a few
days later. As usual, he listened more than he talked.

We liked what you had to say at the commission meeting last week, Mr. Stone said.

Sheridan said politely, May I know who "we" are?

Ah, Mr. Stone said with a chuckle. "We" are a very
progressive investment fund. We look at new opportunities, especially in the natural resources area, and try to
direct our investors and others toward specific development
projects. We have studied the Southern Utes' opportunities
and agree with you completely that the Animas–La Plata
water is crucial to their success. So, we simply wanted to
meet you and offer our support in your efforts.

Sheridan nodded slightly. Very generous of you. Do
you mind if I ask a few questions?

Not at all, Stone chuckled. We're used to hard questions in our business.

Have you met with Chairman Cloud, Leonard Cloud, at the reservation headquarters down in Ignacio? Sheridan asked.

Not yet, young Palmer intervened. But we were hoping you might help arrange an introduction. Stone's lips smiled, but his eyes frowned.

You don't need an introduction from me, Sheridan said. The Utes have been waiting for people with money to show up for quite a few years now. Problem is, now that they're trying to take control of their own resources, a whole lot of folks like you are showing up. Don't mean to be impolite, but it's the truth.

Stone said, Exactly. But that's why we thought having you open the door might make a big difference. We've done a good deal of homework, "due diligence" we call it, and we know of your extraordinary position with the tribe, Mr. Sheridan.

Shaking his head, Sheridan said, I don't have any "position," let alone an "extraordinary" one. They were my father's friends, and my grandfather's before him, and so they're my friends too. Nothing extraordinary about it. He paused. And by the way, I don't trade on friendships, extraordinary or not.

Oh, no, no, no, Stone said quickly. Nothing of the kind. Both men shook their heads vigorously. We simply meant that a call from you to Chairman Cloud, or better yet, if you came along with us, would offer a kind of...credibility, if I may use that word, that we might not otherwise have and others certainly would not have.

By credibility, Sheridan said, I gather you mean a head start, an advantage. Over the "others." He pushed his unfinished lunch back and leaned back in his chair. Let's see if I understand what's going on here. Your investment fund—what do you call it?

Nature's Capital, young Palmer offered helpfully, pulling a business card from his pocket.

Sheridan said, I see. Nature's Capital wants to help the Utes develop their resources—methane coal gas right now, and oil and natural gas to come—so that they can, what did you say, "provide a better life for those too long left out of modern" something.

Advancement, young Palmer said eagerly.

Advancement, Sheridan repeated. And you need my help to do that.

Not exactly "need," Stone interrupted. Would like to have, is a better way of putting it. He now pushed his card across the table at Sheridan. A kind of partnership. Win-win-win. We win by financing Ute energy projects. The Utes win by finally enjoying the benefits of the resources God gave them. And you win—

It wasn't God, Sheridan interrupted.

What? Stone asked, I thought—

It was good old Uncle Sam, Sheridan said, a note of keen intensity in his voice. God didn't put the Utes down there in that wind-blasted desert. Uncle Sam did. The US government did. We did, he said, pointing at Stone, young Palmer, and himself. We put them there about a hundred and thirty years ago. And you know what? We left them there. We forgot about them. We couldn't have cared less. And then, guess what, the Arabs decided they didn't want us to get their oil for fifty cents a barrel and shut the valves. All of a sudden, "we" needed to find oil fast. Guess where "we" looked? On their land. And "we" found oil and gas there. And you know what happened next? The good old US Department of the Interior, Bureau of goddamn Indian Affairs, leased the rights to the oil and gas to major oil companies—he dropped his voice to a whisper—and gave the Utes spare change. A pittance. A fraction of the profits. Embarrassingly little.

Though he had not raised his voice, Sheridan's face had darkened. Under the table, his hands shook with anger. He now spoke between set teeth. If I were you, I wouldn't go down there with your money and talk about what God gave them. If anything, God played a trick on Uncle Sam. He said to Himself, Let's see, the white men are putting the red men in the corner of a desert, more or less to get rid of them, while the land they roamed is taken from them. But these same white men, God says to Himself, are putting oil in cars and burning it up real fast. So, let's even things out. I've put a lot of that oil under the land used to corral the red men and now we'll see what happens when the white men need it.

Sheridan leaned across the table. Some people call that Divine Justice. Me? I don't know whether it's divine or not. But it sure as hell is justice.

Both men were now still. They both shook their heads slowly. Young Palmer's eyes were wide and apprehensive. Stone then nodded thoughtfully, as if viewing a particularly complex balance sheet. I see, he said. Good advice. Very good advice. Thank you for that. We'll be, shall I say, careful in that regard.

You don't have to worry about Chairman Cloud, Sheridan said. He's served in the US Air Force and even did a few years at the BIA—Bureau of Indian Affairs—so he knows what's going on. And you'll find him much less, what should I say, intense on this subject than I am. He's a very smart man and I'm sure he'll listen politely to what you have to say. He has quite a number of new friends these days, especially in your line of work.

Which brings us back, Stone said, to the matter of your...involvement. We really do value your advice and, as we have said, think having you on our side would make a great deal of difference in our success with the Southern Ute Tribe. They will, after all, need financing to develop their resources, that is if the courts confirm that those resources are theirs. I mentioned win-win. You would win, possibly big, as well.

We'll see what the courts do pretty quickly, Sheridan said. The Utes have Sammy Maynard, and he's one of the best. Been with them since Chairman Cloud became leader in the sixties. He paused and looked out of the partially opened window at the street below. You have the wrong man, Sheridan said, where "winning" is concerned. I don't have much beside my own land, my family's land, and I never will. And if I haven't already made it clear, then I will. I don't trade in friendships. If you're talking about some sort of reward for joining your team, what do you call yourselves?

Nature's Capital, young Palmer said quietly.

Nature's Capital, Sheridan repeated. Anyway, I'll just say no thanks. It's not how I do business.

At that point Stone lowered his voice, scanned the room, and said, Mr. Sheridan, there is considerable talk around here, and I gather in other parts of Colorado, that you might be interested in seeking a statewide office. Some even say the governorship.

Sheridan stared at him, eyes narrowed.

I have no idea, Stone continued, whether that is true or not true. But what I do know is that seeking public office these days, what with media and consultants and whatnot, is very costly. Now, you yourself have said that you are not a man of means. So, if you have an interest in serving in a higher capacity, and I have no doubt you would do so with great skill and integrity—I've seen how you handle yourself in the county commissioners' meetings—you'll need financial resources. A rather large amount of financial resources.

Sheridan's gaze narrowed, disconcertingly, further.

Let's just say that we at Nature's Capital—and by the way, we are a subsidiary of one of the largest investment banks in the country—would do all we could to see that you had the resources necessary to carry out those ambitions.

Sheridan was silent. He pushed his unfinished lunch plate away farther. Then he pushed their respective business cards back toward them. He stood and said, Gentlemen, whether I do or do not seek another public office should have nothing to do with your efforts to make money off the Utes, and it won't. If I were to run for higher office, in fact, it would be specifically to prevent that kind of corruption. You do whatever you wish with the Utes. They're smart enough to know who to trust and who not to. They've had a lot of experience in that regard. Just don't use my name in any of your dealings with them.

That all happened some years ago. But what transpired thereafter would become part of the Sheridan legend in those parts.

7.

After his Monday coffee with his local Monday and Friday group and then another cup with Ms. Chandler, Sheridan walked across the street to his pickup. Near the vehicle stood a tall, angular young man in standard student wear: jeans and a work shirt.

Mr. Sheridan? the young man asked. Sheridan nodded. May I speak with you?

Sheridan nodded again. Surely. About what?

The young man coughed. My name is Pat Carroll. I was a student of Professor Smithson, you know, Duane Smithson. Sheridan nodded again, and Carroll continued, I studied history with him and I may go on and get a graduate degree at Boulder or somewhere in modern history and teach. Right now I'm interning at the *Durango Herald,* at least through the summer.

Where you from? Sheridan asked.

Well, my dad was involved in government, the young man said, and I've lived here, studied at Fort Lewis, for most of my life. He paused. I like it here. A lot.

Sheridan nodded again. What exactly can I do for you, Mr. Carroll?

Pat—Patrick, the young man said. I was wondering if I could talk to you about a story. For the paper. The *Herald.*

What kind of story? Sheridan asked warily.

It's a kind of, I guess you'd say, a kind of profile, the young man said.

Profile of what? Sheridan asked.

The young man avoided Sheridan's steady gaze. Well, it's…it's about…what I had in mind was to write something about...you.

Sheridan shook his head. I don't think so, but I appreciate the interest, he said. He turned to open the pickup door.

The young man said, But Mr. Sheridan, I've read all the stories in our paper—

Sheridan said, Well, as newspapers go, the *Herald*'s not bad. But I'd encourage you not to believe everything you read. Ink and paper don't make it so.

I don't mean to be pushy, Mr. Sheridan, the young man stuttered. But you're interesting. You've had an interesting life. You've come up in conversations with Professor Smithson. You've had a really interesting life...but most people around here think you're kind of a...a mystery of some kind. So, I thought—

Let's leave it a mystery, shall we? Sheridan said as he got in the truck. I like it that way.

That Friday, he joined the group at the coffee shop, and after the usual survey of current gossip and world events, the professor took him aside. Dan, he said, I think you met my student, Patrick Carroll.

I did indeed, Sheridan said. Was this "profile" idea his or yours?

His, the professor said. All his. He's very bright. Straight As. Besides, he's actually the late Congressman Carroll's son. And he's quickly tired of covering the garden clubs and weddings and writing the obituaries. And he's picked a few things up and—

Sheridan shook his head vigorously. I liked old Congressman Carroll, and I was wondering if the young man might be junior. But even so, we don't want to do that, Duane. Not now. Not never. You've got to tell him it's just not going to happen. You understand. I know you understand.

What if he stayed away from...you know...the bad part? the professor said.

There's no "bad part," Sheridan said. There's a complicated part. And for my money, it'll stay complicated well after I'm six feet under up at the end of Florida Road. And then no one reading the *Durango Herald* or anything else is going to give a good damn. Matter of fact, they don't give a good damn now. And you have to tell this young man, Mr. Carroll, that that's a fact.

He's read all the old stories already, the professor said. You know, he went back into the *Herald* morgue—

That's the right name, Sheridan interrupted. Right where these old stories should stay.

—and he says the stories at the time don't make sense. He says that the whole thing stinks. Smithson studied Sheridan's face. He says what happened was not right. It was unfair. I think Patrick even said it was unjust.

Well, Duane—Sheridan looked away—stink or no stink, I'm not talking about it. That's just the way it is... and that's the way it's gonna be. Why in the world would you or anyone else think I want to talk to some college kid years later about that nightmare?

I know, the professor said. I know. I told him that, but he's got a burr under his saddle about it and he's damned determined. I can't talk him out of it.

He's gonna have to get rid of that burr on his own. 'Cause he's not talking to me. Sheridan looked at his friend. There's other people involved here, and even if I wanted to stir up that whole nasty business, I don't have the right to do that to them. You know that.

The professor had known Sheridan since his first campaign for county commissioner, and Sheridan occasionally had a quiet dinner with the Smithson family. Smithson had witnessed the events that brought upheaval to Sheridan's life, though he had never known, and would never ask about, details that had never come to light.

If I didn't know you better, Duane, I'd think you might have put this young man up to this. Sheridan looked at him steadily. But I know you'd never do that.

The professor shook his head forcefully. Dan, I'd never do that. You know that.

I do, Duane, I do. But I'm gonna have to ask you to call young Mr. Carroll off. Give him a new project. Have him do one of these profile things on Mr. Cloud. He's a lot more interesting—and important—than I ever was.

Actually, that's the project I proposed to Pat. He was doing his research for a long story on Leonard, and he found your tracks all over the place. But the more he tried to put the pieces together, the less sense he could make of it all.

He wouldn't be the first, now would he? Sheridan asked.

He's not my student anymore, Dan, the professor said. I'll do what I can to call him off. But he's not necessarily going to do what I ask him.

He can do what he wants, Sheridan said. But he's not getting any help from me. You do what you can to help him understand that. And, by the way, I can say with authority that there's one or two other people he hadn't ought to be talking to either.

The professor watched Sheridan retreating down Main Avenue and knew very well he meant Caroline Chandler.

8.

The following Saturday night, Caroline looked out her kitchen window and saw Sheridan's dusty red pickup truck even before she heard it coming up her road. Like Sheridan, she had a gate, and the locals by custom honored the privacy those gates requested.

He took off his hat and grinned as he set the quart whiskey bottle down. You got ice, he asked, or is your freezer broken again?

She started past him, and he firmly grasped her wrist. She looked at him at close range, then gave him a lingering kiss on the lips.

Well, doesn't that ever heal a broken day, he said.

Your day broken? she asked as she poured the drinks.

Not now it isn't, he said.

Well, then, she said, that just makes my job that much easier.

No job from me, he chuckled, unless you're lookin' for one.

She waved him to the corner kitchen table and set the drinks down. Sheridan scratched her frisky Irish setter pup behind the ear as it sniffed Toby's scent on his Levis. What're you up to nowadays? he asked.

Just waitin' for little chicks to hatch, she said over the top of her glass, and prayin' for sinners.

Sheridan laughed. Well, now, that's a full-time job all by itself. Any particular sinners, or you prayin' for all of us?

Just you, Daniel. She smiled warmly. You require about all the prayers I've got.

Let me ask you something, Ms. Caroline. They tapped

glasses, and he took a hefty sip and said, Ahhh. Do you think Leonard and the Utes are doing the right thing with this trust fund they've set up? Like any big family that's just won the lottery, they're beginning to fall out amongst themselves over what to take and what to save. I'd hate to see a donnybrook down there over all this money.

She thought, then said, I believe he knows exactly what he's doing, and he's brought in some sound advisors, from what I can tell.

In her earlier years, first in New York, then in Denver, she had been a rising star in the investment banking community and was known to have done some creative investment deals and made a very comfortable income in the process.

As you advised, she continued, I did get on my horse and go see Leonard. We had a long talk and he laid out the structure of the tribal trust and the conditions on its use he got the tribal council to adopt. It's a pretty solid arrangement and should carry them for a couple of generations or more. I suggested some provisions for individuals to cash out at current dollar terms. But if they do, they forfeit participation in the future proceeds. A few of them, a couple of the young hotheads, are taking off. But it looks like the large majority are sitting tight.

He nodded. That's what I'd hoped. It'd be a shame if they fell apart and started quarreling.

She took a drink of the Jameson and said, You been down to see Two Hawks lately? She knew that he did so from time to time, and there were very few secrets on the reservation. I hear he's still very respected, even among the younger ones.

He nodded again. Yeah, I dropped in on him. But we didn't get into the money stuff.

She waited.

His large glass was now half empty, the ice melting quickly. It's strange, he said finally. After I've spent an hour or so with him, I'm kinda lighthearted, or as much so as I ever was. And I have a—don't laugh, now—I have a really powerful feeling about the spirits at work in the natural world. He's got some strong medicine inside him. Sheridan gestured toward his heart. I've never understood it, but it's always like that. Far be it from me to declare who's holy and who's not. But if anyone is, that old man is.

She got up, looked in the oven, and brought the whiskey bottle back to the table. She poured the width of a finger or two in each. This was the hour she treasured with Sheridan. Presently, she said, I went to see him too, Daniel.

He looked surprised.

I have a number of times, she continued. Pretty much for the same reason as you. It's very hard to explain and I'd never even try with anyone but you. Don't worry, she said, we don't talk about you.

This was largely, but not totally, true. She and Two Hawks never discussed Sheridan by name. But they both referred to "our friend" from time to time and walked carefully around his soul.

Caroline got up and brought plates and old silver to the table. He is holy somehow, she said. You couldn't explain this to anyone who hadn't known him a long time. It just sounds like some kind of Hollywood Indian talk. But he is. I'm pretty much awestruck when I'm with him. And like you just said, you come away better and…I guess…healthier, somehow.

You're the healthiest person I know, Sheridan said. She laughed. He said, No, I really mean it. You're always on an even keel. I haven't seen you mad in…well, a pretty long time. You seem content with what you've got. He smiled, Am I wrong?

She shook her head. No, you're not wrong. I've been luckier than most. Ingratitude is a sin, and not one I'm about to commit. She took a large sip of whiskey and looked evenly at him. She stood up again and said, I save my sins for other things. She removed a baked chicken from the oven and brought it and a pan of roasted potatoes to the table. This going to be enough? she asked.

Beggars can't be choosers, Sheridan said. Well, now Ms. Missionary Lady, we going to have a prayer meeting or should I carve this bird? He started carving without waiting for a response.

Didn't mean to wander off into theology, Caroline said. It's just that I'm grateful for all that I have… She hesitated, then laid a hand on his arm. Including you here tonight, she said. He raised her hand to his lips and kissed it. Me too, he said softly.

Early the next morning, she awoke with a start. The bedroom was cold, the windows customarily open. Though she knew what she would not find, she reached across the bed. His place was still warm. She sighed and ran a hand through her hair. She turned over and slept until the sun came through the window to wake her again.

She went downstairs and foggily started to make coffee. Then she realized he had started it before leaving. She smiled and shook her head. She watched jays razzing each other over the bird feeder outside the kitchen window. Then she poured the strong coffee into a thick, worn mug and went to the table.

There sat an object wrapped in plain brown paper. It was a foot or so tall, and she knew immediately what it was. She held the object and hesitated. Finally, she tore away the string and paper. It was another carving for her collection. She probably had a half dozen or more. This was an Indian figure holding what appeared to be a bird, a raptor, probably a hawk, to his chest.

She held it against her breast. A single tear made its way down her cheek.

9.

A few evenings later, another dinner took place on the outskirts of Durango. After the dessert dishes were cleared, Mrs. Farnsworth took her young guest into the comfortable sitting room.

Patrick, she began, I'll tell you most of what I know. It is certainly not everything that happened. Probably no more than two people know all that happened then. And I'm not one of them. But as a newspaperwoman, I'm going to do so on ground rules I don't like and I'd advise you never to use. When you interview someone, particularly a public official, they should always be on the record. Don't let anyone give you this "off the record" stuff.

Patrick Carroll said, But Mrs. Farnsworth, this is about a public official. So, shouldn't even what *you* say be quotable?

No, she insisted, it shouldn't. At least not in this case. Most of what I'll tell you is already public record. Whether it is *accurate* public record is another matter, and you'll have to decide that. He nodded.

But there is one other thing, Patrick, she continued. Even if you solve the mystery, as you see it, I cannot guarantee I'll run your profile. That's for me, and me alone, to decide. In fact, I'll tell you right now, I probably *won't* run it.

He frowned. Then he said, Could we leave that decision until you see what I come up with?

She didn't respond. Here's what happened, at least as I remember it, she said. Fifteen or more years ago, there was a terrific struggle going on over the degree to which the Indian tribes had the legal right to develop their own resources. The Southern Utes were in some respects in the lead. Up to that point, the Bureau of Indian Affairs negotiated leases with major energy companies and paid the tribes a pretty small royalty. Certainly nothing like what the resources were worth. The matter was brought to a head both by the foreign oil embargoes in the 1970s and, consequently, by the sharp rise in oil prices. Suddenly lots of money was at stake, and several lawsuits were filed against the US government and the oil companies to test the issue of whether the natural resources on tribal lands—reservations—belonged to the US government or to the respective tribes.

Patrick was writing all this down, or trying to. She waved a hand at him. You can find all this on the Internet and in quite a number of books and articles from that period. Ultimately, one of the cases—not the Southern Utes' case—got to the Supreme Court, as it was almost bound to. This was a landmark issue. When the tribes got parked on reservations after the Civil War, everyone just took for granted that they were poor and would always stay

poor. And likewise that anything valuable on those reservations belonged to us—she gestured at herself and Patrick—
us white people.

Even better than the Internet, she continued, if this
interests you, go see Sam Maynard and his partners. They've
been up to their eyeballs in this from the beginning. The
basic point is that the Indians, the Utes particularly, were
now recognized to have, for the first time in their troubled
history, real wealth. It was already established that there
was oil and gas and some coal and even uranium on the
Southern Utes' land. And you don't have to be as old as I
am to know what happened next. The vultures filled the
skies around here.

What were they after? Patrick looked puzzled. The
vultures...?

Frances Farnsworth laughed. Money vultures, Patrick.
Money vultures. People who called themselves investment
bankers. They were all over the Utes like a massive blanket.
Here were a bunch of unsophisticated, only partially edu-
cated people, and they needed financial "advisors," people
who would tell them how to manage their resources and
new wealth. For fees, of course. Very large fees.

Patrick held up his hand. And Mr. Sheridan was still a
county commissioner then?

He was, she said. And very close to Leonard Cloud
and his lawyer, Sam Maynard. The New York money people figured that out pretty quickly. They're not rich by accident. So Daniel—Mr. Sheridan—was a popular fellow in
those days.

I know for a fact he chased one of the first groups
away, she continued. And, from what I heard, they were

not amused. He was pretty…what should I say…*direct* with them. Word soon got around in those circles that Mr. Sheridan was a tough cookie. Nevertheless, efforts continued to be made by several of these…interest groups, shall we say, to enlist his services. All on behalf of the benighted Indians, of course. But this was always accompanied by mention of handsome fees for his service in intermediating with the tribe. She rose and filled their coffee cups.

So, how did all the trouble start? Patrick asked.

The trouble had already started when Mr. Sheridan walked away—stalked away would probably be a better description—from the first investors. They called themselves Nature's Capital or some such, but that was just a new smokescreen created by a giant financial conglomerate. She laughed. We taxpayers had to bail them out a year or so ago and they still collapsed.

Patrick said, This is where the trail gets confused. So, what happened then?

What happened then, she said, looking at the ceiling of her Victorian sitting room, was that the knives came out for Mr. Sheridan. As you know, he had earned a state-wide reputation for helping work out a compromise on the Animas–La Plata project, with recognition of the interests of the Utes, and he had been called in to arbitrate a series of long-standing water disputes around the state. He had made himself something of an expert by then and was getting all kinds of invitations to speak at water congresses and other such events where crowds of one kind or another were conferencing. In those days he was—for that matter still is—a pretty impressive figure. He didn't sound like a politician—still doesn't—primarily because he wasn't one.

She studied her hands, remembering. He was the best we had produced for a long time, she said quietly.

And people back then were beginning to talk about him for some office, Patrick said. I gather governor or something.

Indeed, Mrs. Farnsworth said. And a committee was formed here to begin to organize support around the state. Mr. Maynard, Mr. Murphy, your professor Smithson, and a number of other people signed up. Mr. Sheridan didn't encourage them. But he didn't exactly discourage them either. As I recall, he treated it with considerable amusement.

Mrs. Farnsworth sipped her coffee and retreated into memory. She and her late husband, Murray, had moved to Durango almost forty years before. They were both from prominent New York families but decided the haute society was not for them. They bought the *Durango Herald*—they had always wanted to run a newspaper—and raised their children in southwestern Colorado. "Pillars of the community" was, in their case, an apt description. They were sophisticated easterners who very shortly let their hair down and became down-to-earth fixtures in the community, on a first-name basis with all. Though old-style moderate Republicans, they pitched their editorials, each taking turns, right down the middle, which was where most southwestern Coloradans liked their political pitches. Anyone who felt the need or had the use for a firearm should be able to own one, or several. And most did. But any woman in need of an abortion should be able to have one also. And occasionally, she chuckled to herself, they even weighed in on the need for arms control agreements between the US and the Soviet Union in the old Cold War days, giving vent to what the Farnsworths called, between themselves, the

Republic of Durango's foreign policy.

Patrick brought her back from her memories. So, he said, Mr. Sheridan was maneuvering—

Being maneuvered, she corrected.

—being maneuvered into a candidacy for governor, the vultures were circling—

And some of them landing, she added.

—and some of them landing. And then the roof fell in on Sheridan.

As our paper reported, she said, he was accused of accepting payment, taking bribes, for using his county commission office—by then he was chairman of the commission—for arranging financial contracts with the Southern Ute Tribe. Naturally, he denied it and opened his account at the Bank of Durango to prove it. His accusers promptly responded that there were other banks, including in Switzerland or the Cayman Islands, where money could be readily deposited.

That means he had to prove a negative, Patrick exclaimed.

Exactly, she responded.

They must have had some other evidence.

There were two members of the tribal council who offered to testify that he had given them money to support a bid by a large and powerful investment fund to manage the tribe's resource development projects. They opened their bank accounts, new ones, and there the money was in the amount they claimed he gave them.

That's not enough evidence to convict him, Patrick nearly shouted.

Ah, Patrick. Young man. You don't know our man Mr. Sheridan. He was—he is—an old-fashioned man of honor. His honor is more important to him than that land he got from his father, or his horse, or his dog, or his pickup truck, or just about anything else. He did not intend to have his honor besmirched. He resigned from the La Plata County Commission and ordered his friends to close down the blossoming political campaign. He simply went back up to the top of Florida Road, and that's where he's been ever since.

Patrick shook his head. I don't know, Mrs. Farnsworth, there's something else here. There were all kinds of other dark insinuations around this time, including in the *Herald*. There seemed to be other things going on as well. That's what I'm trying to find out about. No one wants to talk about it.

Almost exactly at this time, she said, studying him directly, we received a letter—Murray and I—at the paper. It alleged in considerable detail that Mr. Sheridan had accepted the payments, and distributed them, because he needed the money to pay blackmail.

Blackmail! Patrick's eyes widened.

You are not going to write this, Patrick. At least you are not going to write it for my newspaper, she said.

Blackmail for what? he stammered.

The letter said that he was having an affair with the wife of a prominent man. A very prominent man. And that Mr. Sheridan needed the payoff money to keep the blackmailer from disclosing this.

That's crazy, Patrick said. Nobody cares about that kind of stuff anymore.

They did then, Patrick. And that wasn't too long ago in years. But it was a century ago in public attitudes. She paused and looked out into her garden, studying the bright moonlit flowers. Besides, now someone else's reputation was at stake, not just his own. He's old-fashioned in many ways, our Mr. Sheridan. He believed, I'm sure still does, that a man has a duty to protect the honor of a woman if her honor is brought into question. The letter said the alleged blackmailer was threatening to disclose her name.

Did you show him the letter? Patrick asked.

Didn't have to, she said. By this time he had resigned from office and retreated into private life and whoever wrote the letter had achieved his purpose.

"*His* purpose," you said.

Yes, his purpose. Mrs. Farnsworth studied his face. *His* purpose. Because Murray and I were convinced—though we couldn't prove it—that the husband of the woman in question wrote the defaming letter to destroy Mr. Sheridan. And for all public purposes, Mr. Sheridan was destroyed.

You know who it was, don't you, Patrick stated.

Yes, she said. The woman was Caroline Chandler.

10.

Twelve years earlier, shortly after poking his finger in the eye of the Nature's Capital officials, Dan Sheridan had invited Leonard Cloud to have breakfast at the café that would shortly become the venue of the Monday and Friday coffee club.

Leonard, he had said, I'd be very careful about how you handle these East Coast money types that are showing up. Sheridan related the story of his confrontational lunch with the Nature's Capital men, leaving out much of the conclusion and departing confrontation.

The tribal chairman said, Dan, I understand what's going on now and what will continue to go on until we get ourselves established. Mr. Maynard may be a small-town Durango lawyer, but he's very shrewd where these money men are concerned. Besides, word got around about your wrestling match with the big wallets.

Leonard Cloud and Sam Maynard had played high school basketball against each other, and in one of his first moves after he was selected tribal chairman in the late 1960s, the young Cloud had selected Maynard as tribal attorney. They had now been attorney and client, and close friends, for twenty-five years or more. But in the presence of any third party, including friends of both, they referred to each other in professional terms. Sam Maynard was never known to refer to the Southern Ute chairman as anything other than Mr. Cloud.

Well, I suspected you'd be covering your six, Sheridan said, knowing the Ute chairman would understand the combat pilot reference from his US Air Force days.

Leonard Cloud chuckled. Haven't heard that term in awhile.

Tell me what you have in mind to do with the resource revenues, Sheridan asked, in case it's any of my business.

Of course it is, Dan, Cloud said. How we manage this situation will be important to La Plata County and Durango. Mr. Maynard and I have discussed creating a new tribal investment fund, a kind of trust for ourselves and future generations. The council has agreed that these minerals—these riches—don't belong to just us. We have a responsibility to our kids, and their kids, and many generations to come.

Some of your folks will want to have a party, a pretty big party I'd imagine, Sheridan said. And given your history, it's pretty easy to understand why.

Cloud said, My job—the council's job—is to convince them that the party has to be one where we improve our houses and schools and hospital first. Once we get a decent roof over everyone's head and pay our teachers and nurses better, there'll be enough for singing and dancing. First things first.

Sheridan nodded. He wasn't surprised. Leonard Cloud was one of the most thoughtful individuals he'd ever met.

Cloud continued, We're not the only ones who are going to be romanced. Your story about that New York outfit is just the first. They'll be all over the local officials. Yourself and the county commission and the city council. You're going to get a lot of arguments about how you have to supervise us and look after us poor dumb Indians so we don't all get drunk and tear the place up.

I can handle that, Sheridan said. The rest of the commissioners can too.

After breakfast they got in Cloud's pickup, even dustier than Sheridan's, and drove the twenty miles or so down to Ignacio. Whatever money was on its way, Sheridan noted, had yet to be spent on reservation improvements. Much of the territory was open, undeveloped, and possessed but little in the way of growing things. Ignacio, the tribal headquarters, was home to only a few shops and stores and not much affected by late-twentieth-century progress.

Cloud drove up and down the dusty streets, pointing out where a new grade school would be built and where the modest hospital, not much more than a clinic, would be substantially expanded. Sheridan imagined his friend's visions of up-to-date medical equipment, full-scale surgery capabilities, and treatment for the routine illnesses of a denied people. As they passed, Sheridan and Cloud recognized familiar faces and gave solemn waves.

As Cloud drove him back to Durango, Sheridan said, Leonard, something tells me the politics of this revolution are not going down quietly. Too much at stake. I have a terrible feeling some people are going to get trampled by this stampede before it's all over.

Cloud nodded in agreement. I'm concerned about our people. But some of you people there in Durango better be careful as well. We have a saying that there's no clear skies without a storm first.

11.

Water and energy finally came together for the Southern Utes in the 1980s and 1990s, with the help of Congress and the federal courts. The semidormant Animas–La Plata water project could not by now justify itself solely on traditional agricultural economic grounds. Theoretically, at least, the federal Bureau of Reclamation had to make the semblance of a case for any new dam on the grounds that it would repay its costs through stimulation of agricultural development. Despite Reclamation's exploration of elaborate pump-storage methods, whereby water would be pumped from the Animas to a high storage reservoir and then released when needed for crops and consumers, the economics of the Animas–La Plata project were making increasingly less sense.

Then federal energy policy began to change in response to OPEC oil embargoes of the late 1970s. And Indian tribes began to assert their rights to control their own energy resources and to demand fair treatment where water resources were concerned. In 1974 the Southern Utes, partly under the advice of their attorney, Sam Maynard, demanded a moratorium on the development of their vast natural gas deposits, and a year later they joined a consortium of two dozen Indian tribes in forming CERT, the Council of Energy Resource Tribes. Almost everything about Native American tribes involves a certain degree of irony, and CERT, modeled on the OPEC consortium that had brought the US economy to its knees, was no different. In contrast to its Persian Gulf model, however, it represented the original Americans who now laid claim to energy supplies under their largely forsaken reservations.

In response, in 1982 Congress passed the Indian Mineral Development Act, acknowledging the authority of the various tribes to negotiate their own mineral leases without the oversight of the Department of the Interior and its Bureau of Indian Affairs. Coincidentally, that same year the Supreme Court ruled that the Apache Tribe had the right to impose a severance tax on oil and gas produced from its land. For an energy-rich tribe like the Southern Utes, this judicial decision greatly expanded its potential revenue base.

Almost simultaneously, Indian water rights were being addressed by the federal government as well. In 1988, Congress took up the Indian Water Rights Settlement Act, which sought to resolve age-old disputes about what water rights, if any, Indian tribes were entitled to. Colorado, like certain other Western states, had early on adopted the so-called appropriation doctrine—shorthanded as "first in time, first in right"—to determine water rights during the frontier days. This doctrine evolved over decades into a complex system for guaranteeing water rights based on who got there first and how much they used. It did not, however, resolve the rights of those who had been using water for centuries before the white man trekked west on his horse and in his covered wagon.

After considerable deliberation, the Southern Utes agreed to forgo their senior water rights in exchange for water from the stalemated Animas–La Plata project. This had the sudden and unexpected effect of substantially altering the economics of the project and giving it a whole new lease on life. Virtually overnight, a lot of farmers, developers, and local boosters discovered the Southern Utes as their new best friends. One writer in a newspaper called *Westword* summed up this revolution with these words: "Conservative white farmers and ranchers, as well as 'good ol' boy' developers in Durango, started championing Native American rights like born liberals."

So, with energy and water reaching a dynamic political mix, Southern Ute tribal chairman Leonard Cloud and his council created their own resource development company in 1992 using funds received from the federal government under the Colorado Ute Indian Water Rights Settlement

Agreement. They called the company Red Willow. In 1995 the Southern Utes assumed ownership of fifty-four natural gas wells, and they increased production fourfold in less than a year. Unlike private production companies, which were required to pay property and severance taxes to the state and county and income taxes to the federal government, the tribe was exempt from these taxes and thus would reap substantially larger profits on these and future projects.

After more than a century of virtual isolation, within a decade or so the Southern Utes found themselves in the modern commercial world and able to command much of their own destiny. If not overnight, then figuratively close to it, they had emerging wealth, social status, and political importance. Now, when all-party discussions about the Animas–La Plata project were held, tribal representatives were near the head of the table. When plans for future economic development in La Plata County and southwestern Colorado were being drawn up, Leonard Cloud or his representatives were invited as full partners.

And throughout the 1970s and beyond, Leonard Cloud and other tribal officials, largely at the urging of Sam Maynard, were periodic visitors to Washington. They arranged visits with their Colorado congressional delegation to seek support in their late dependency days and even more so during and after the water and energy revolutions that greatly elevated their status.

Eventually the Utes acquired principled and dedicated professional financial advice, and Maynard could call on other top-flight legal experts as required. During the heady transition days, however, the vultures did circle, as Dan

Sheridan's experience proved. It was by no means certain in the late 1970s and 1980s that the Utes would not be picked over and picked apart by the emerging army of the unscrupulous.

Sheridan's concern throughout that time was for his friend Leonard Cloud and the tribe his grandfather had befriended in the late nineteenth century. He felt it was somehow symbolic that the Florida River that arose above the ancestral Sheridan ranch as a small rivulet and flowed through it as a somewhat larger stream united with the Animas River below Ignacio on the Southern Ute reservation. The Animas was the major artery for not only Durango but also those early mining towns of Silverton and Ouray above it to the north. The Florida had been dammed to create the Lemon Reservoir just below the Sheridan ranch and was the somewhat smaller artery for ranchers to the northeast of Durango. Durango did not share in the waters stored in the Lemon Reservoir, but the Utes did.

From his earliest days with his father, Sheridan had fly-fished the Florida from its banks on his own land and above and below and eventually in the Lemon Reservoir. You could not be a westerner without deep, almost profound appreciation for the importance of that water to virtually all life—to the deep-rooted ponderosa pines that could get their tentacles near its moisture, to the wildflowers it helped nourish, to the cattle and the farmers down below where the land leveled out, to his grandmother, who in her earlier pioneer days carried buckets from the stream for all the household needs.

Occasionally Sheridan reflected that his family and the Utes shared the same water. He left his bedroom window open in all weather so that he could hear the waters surging and gurgling on their way south. He knew the Florida, like the Animas and all other creeks, streams, and rivers in western Colorado, indeed throughout the West, were derived from the snow in the high country—in his case, the 14,000-plus-foot mountains in the Weminuche Wilderness Area, part of the great San Juan National Forest in the San Juan Mountains to his north and east.

Though some of the forest in the San Juans could be timbered under management by the US Forest Service, the Weminuche, named after one of the original Ute bands, was now permanently set aside from development or use other than for recreation. Its extraordinary wild natural beauty could be hiked and camped. But its resources were preserved, and no motor would violate its stillness. As a boy Sheridan had hiked it first with his father, then with high school friends, then in middle and later years more often by himself. The Weminuche was as close to a cathedral as he would need to get.

On some occasions, he and Caroline had put panniers on a spare packhorse and camped out in the Weminuche. The wilderness had been his escape to safety in the bad days. He guessed others might call it a refuge. The wilderness had saved his life, he reflected on more than one occasion. Or at least his sanity.

In recent years he had also reflected on more than one occasion that it might not be a bad place in which to die.

12.

All this local history was well known to the Monday and Friday coffee club, if for no other reason than that Sam Maynard kept the group filled in on developments in the far-off corridors of economic and judicial power. The politics of it all they could pretty well figure out for themselves.

On the occasion that Leonard Cloud joined them, he would, in his laconic manner, keep them up to date on tribal developments. Given that most tribal council meetings were open to the public, the *Durango Herald* faithfully carried next-day stories of its deliberations. Less well known were the behind-the-scenes dealings with financiers, boosters, and fast-buck pitchmen. And, of course, that was where most of the drama occurred.

On a Friday morning after the Utes' fortunes changed, Mr. Murphy had said, I always had high regard for Mr. Cloud. But I have to say, the way he's handling all this oil and gas and coal money they're about to get is pretty shrewd.

Shrewd isn't the word for it, the professor said. He's a regular financial wizard. Future generations of Utes will honor his name.

Maybe we oughta send him to Washington...as president or something, Bill Van Ness said. That idea amused them.

Could do a whole lot worse, Sheridan suggested.

And we no doubt will, Mr. Murphy offered. Laughter all around.

Sam Maynard said, They're not home free yet, by any means. The Southern Ute Tribe now has investments in office buildings in Denver and even farther on and energy projects all over the place. They got to be careful. They're still learning that markets can go down as well as up.

Bill Van Ness said, We all had to learn that one, now didn't we? There were nods all around. What do they call their company?

Sam said, Red Willow. But now there are Red Willow subsidiaries sprouting all over the place.

Mr. Murphy winked when Sam's head was turned. They'll be hiring some big-shot Denver law firms, I suspect, he said. Maybe even New York ones. Big-time corporations like that need those fancy lawyers.

Sam smiled and said, We'll see. Mr. Cloud remembers who helped him when. They've always paid their legal bills. But back when, sometimes they had to wait awhile.

What was that case where that big old oil company had to pay a fine, Sam? the professor asked.

Sam said, It wasn't exactly a fine. My law firm brought a suit against one of the big oil companies to give the tribe ownership of the methane gas locked up in their big coal deposits. The idea was that if they owned the coal, which by now it was clear they did, then they also had to own the gas trapped in it. And that methane gas was itself worth a fortune. Anyway, they ultimately lost the legal argument. But before they did, the oil company settled with them.

How much did they get? Mr. Murphy asked

Half a billion, Sam said.

Half a what? Van Ness exclaimed.

Billion, Sam said.

Wow, the professor said. Which oil company was that?

It was Amoco, Sam said. But it's not Amoco anymore. It belongs to a giant outfit you may have heard of called

British Petroleum—BP.

Years later, the remaining members of the coffee club would have occasion to remember this conversation after BP tried to fill the Gulf of Mexico with oil.

Sheridan pushed back his chair and bid them goodbye. He collected his aged straw Stetson hat off the tree and waved over his shoulder.

The rest of them drank their coffee for a while. Presently Bill Van Ness said, He usually doesn't like all this talk about money, does he?

After a moment Mr. Murphy said, No, he doesn't very much. But you can't actually blame him. He never was a man for the money talk in any case. Now it's like mentioning rope in the house of a man who's been hanged.

Sheridan drove the familiar route up Florida Road, always pronounced "flor-eye-da" by the locals, past the Lemon Reservoir to his place. His small Hereford herd was in a high meadow a couple of miles above his ranch. He parked the truck and went to the barn to saddle Red, along the way frowning at a couple of loose boards near the weathered barn door and making a note to nail them down and set aside a few days to repaint the barn. Once in the saddle, he let the horse know he wanted to go up the winding meadow trail and then relaxed for the half hour or so it would take him to get there.

More than once he found himself wondering what Caroline would be doing. He supposed she would have packed her easel and paints on her horse and would be up in a similar meadow to the west, sketching and then filling in the deep greens of the pine trees, bright yellows of the quaking aspen leaves and their white tree trunks, the mixed blues, purples, whites, and yellows of the wild mountain flowers and, of course, her favorites, the wild columbines in colors ranging from pale yellow to deep burgundy.

The thought made him smile. As she collected his carvings, he collected her paintings. He must have a half dozen or more throughout the ranch house. His favorite—elk and deer in the meadow where he was headed—hung on the wall opposite his bed. He saw it every morning when he awoke and every late evening before turning out his reading light.

For a while she had not been able to stay at his house overnight. It had become a common occurrence for her to wake him from a dream, he overheated and interrupted in mid-groan, to calm him down. Once or twice, at her insistence, he had told her they were always the same: a chase, a maze, he pursuing or being pursued. What he did not tell her was that she was with him in virtually all of them.

Seeing that painting in the early morning, at or before dawn, always contented him. The mornings were the best, the early hours of the night the worst.

As the big horse methodically climbed the trail, he reflected on the good fortunes of his life—Caroline chief among them—and that brief, chaotic period when it all fell apart. If one was the price of the other, he had long since decided, it was well worth the trade-off.

13.

Going back through the *Herfald* stories of a decade and a half ago for the second time, Patrick still couldn't make the pieces fit—even with the background Mrs. Farnsworth had given him.

After rebuffing more than one set of financiers seeking his help in getting close to the Southern Utes, Daniel Sheridan had accepted a deal with one of the investment banks, paid bribes to at least two tribal council members to encourage their support of this bank's bid to be sole financial advisor to the tribe, carried on an affair with Mrs. Caroline Chandler, been found out by her husband, and had taken the bank's money to pay blackmail to her husband. His complex maze discovered, Sheridan had resigned from the La Plata County Commission and had forgone a promising campaign for governor. That's the way the *Herald,* the Denver papers, and even some national media had portrayed the story.

Patrick's research also revealed a notice some months later of the Chandlers' divorce. There was a one-sentence mention of the previous scandal that the Farnsworths had seemed reluctantly obliged to include in the story. Thereafter in the chronology there was no mention of Mr. Chandler. The young man made a note to try to find out what happened to him. He also began to wonder what kind of man Chandler was, what his interests were, why he might have wanted to destroy Sheridan other than to seek revenge as a wronged husband.

But there were also few mentions of Daniel Sheridan in any community stories thereafter. He searched for Sheridan in the *Herald*'s archives and found only one or two mentions of his presence at a funeral of some prominent figure. Sheridan's only semipublic appearances had been one or two lectures to Professor Smithson's Colorado history class at Fort Lewis College. In each case he had been described as a "third-generation Durangoan." That was all.

Patrick now had pages of questions. Given his position and promising future, why would a man like Dan Sheridan risk it all to make money—particularly since he had already turned down chances to make plenty of money? Even if there had been an affair, and Sheridan had steadfastly denied it, why was it such a big deal back then, when it seemed almost routine in the late twentieth century? Patrick would need to do some research on changing social mores. Was there something about Sheridan's relationship with the Southern Utes, and Leonard Cloud particularly, that had made him a target? The hotshot financial high-rollers had other ways to curry favor with the tribe. Why hadn't Sheridan put up a more vigorous public defense? He had simply walked away, almost without comment. What would have been more important to him than clearing up the record and seeking exoneration?

But the one man who quite possibly—even quite probably—could answer most of these and a myriad of other questions wasn't talking. Patrick's boss had said all that she would say. Professor Smithson had asked him to stop working on the Sheridan profile. Virtually everyone to whom he had mentioned Sheridan's name had said only the most complimentary things about him or had simply said he was entitled to his privacy now. He had found one or two old-timers who still seemed to carry a grudge against Sheridan, whose noses turned up and mouths turned down when Patrick asked them about him. He let us down, was about all they would say.

Patrick wondered if Caroline Chandler might know

some things that she had not revealed and, if so, if she would be willing to discuss them now.

14.

Leonard Cloud had tried to find Dan Sheridan for days after his resignation from the county commission back then. Though reluctant to impose on his old friend's privacy, he had even driven up to the Sheridan ranch on two occasions. But Sheridan was not there. Harv Waldron's son was keeping the place up and looking after the animals. Cloud did note that Toby didn't dash out to greet him, and the big red horse was not in his usual corral.

Sheridan was somewhere up in the Weminuche, the tribal chairman had concluded. He'd come down when it was time to.

Years before, while still in high school, Dan Sheridan had found a small high meadow, no more than a dozen acres, with a small stream forming a natural lake deep in the wilderness. The place was miles off the nearest trail, and that was a remote one. It was totally surrounded by tall ponderosas and was protected on two sides by twenty-foot cliffs. Well trained by woodsmen grandfather and father alike, Sheridan knew to build a fire pit near the lake and well away from the pines. There was a perpetual supply of beetle-kill timber on the ground for firewood. He packed in supplies, strung them from a high limb, and pulled them up high at night. What little food waste there was he buried well away from the campsite to prevent bear visits day or night.

Besides the food he packed in, the stream seemed always to have six- to eight-inch trout eager for his hand-tied flies. He had calculated in his youth that if the country were overrun with aliens of one kind or another he could survive in his secluded hideaway for about as long as he needed to.

And, of course, he had the Winchester he had inherited from his father. Through repeated practice with cans on fence posts, Sheridan had assured himself he could handle bear or cougar so long as they didn't jump him in the night. He had learned the creatures' habits from his father and grandfather. Grandfather Sheridan told endless tales of encounters with the predators hunting his horses or cattle, some virtually on the ranch house doorstep. One of Sheridan's earliest memories—chilling at the time—was hearing the late-night mating scream of the cougar. From time to time over the years, the big cats would venture down near the top of Florida Road, usually very early in the morning or as the sun set, looking for a deer or young elk or even one of Sheridan's calves.

You would see them…and then you wouldn't. You would think you saw one, but then you weren't sure. Once or twice he had passed under a tree without checking above eye level only to hear a deep purring growl. Once he found himself fifteen feet away from a full-grown mountain lion. Its leaping range was thirty feet. Though he knew better, he could not help but look fully into the wide, staring, incredibly wise yellow eyes of the magnificent creature. He never forgot the sense of beauty and strength the great cat possessed.

He had never killed one and hoped he would never have to. Survival would be the only defense for doing so.

And even then, being in the cat's territory might justify some punishment for his trespass.

Leonard Cloud might not know the exact location Sheridan's retreat, but he strongly suspected it would be a remote corner of the Weminuche. After a week or two had passed, Sheridan appeared on his doorstep outside Ignacio. Harv's son said you'd been up to see me, he said.

Cloud took him down the street to a small restaurant and they had a beer. Just wanted to see how you were doing, he said. I also wanted to see if I could help.

Sheridan said, Leonard, I guess I'm not surprised. If anyone around here had thought something along those lines, it would've been you. He looked his friend in the eye and said, I greatly appreciate it.

Way I see it, Cloud said, you've been accused and convicted of something you didn't do. It's not right. You've protected us—this tribe—as well as anyone around here. We've known each other since we were both boys, me younger than you, and there isn't a crooked bone in your body. Those two guys on the council are going to resign, whether they realize it yet or not, and if I have anything to do with it, they'll admit that they're thieves and liars. They got some money alright, but it wasn't from you.

Let it go, Leonard, Sheridan said. I don't want to cause anyone else any trouble. They did what they did, and we have to let it go. Everyone involved just followed the usual script: financial types, newspapers, politicians, people with old grudges, anyone with a Sheridan ax to grind, everyone was just playin' their role. Almost everyone.

Cloud studied him. I don't know Mrs. Chandler very well. But what I do know, I like. She is a real lady. She's spent a lot of time down here doing her painting. What Durango people don't know, maybe even you don't know, is that she has also spent a lot of time volunteering in the grade school and the medical clinic. Many hours, in fact. Many days.

Sheridan swallowed hard. I didn't know it. She's never said. He paused. But I'm not surprised.

It's none of my business, Dan, Cloud said, but I want to help out. You had some legal bills, I know. And you couldn't get your cows to market while all this stuff was going on. We Southern Utes are going to earn a lot of money, and I'd be honored if you'd be a kind of advisor or counselor to the tribal council.

Sheridan shook his head vigorously. Can't do it, Leonard. It wouldn't look right. And it would undoubtedly cause you more controversy and trouble. The press would want to look into it again and some in the tribe and the public would think there was something suspicious. He looked out the window for a time. I can't tell you how much I appreciate it, though, he said. It's a real gesture of friendship.

I'm not surprised, Cloud said. I pretty much suspected what you'd say. But I felt honor-bound to offer.

15.

The long stalemate over the Animas–La Plata project drove already bitter feelings even deeper throughout southwestern Colorado. Instead of seeking compromise, the positions of advocates and opponents alike hardened. Political leaders, long accustomed to addressing the matter with an "on the one hand we need the water, but on the other hand we can't keep building dams everywhere" approach, now found themselves with little if any middle ground to occupy. You were either with the advocates or with the opponents.

Calls for study didn't work anymore, either. The project had been studied to death, almost literally. Pro-development studies were denounced by environmental opponents as biased, and anti-development studies proved many times over that the project could not pay for itself, at least in terms of increased agricultural production.

Being civilized, the people of Durango, especially those who had taken hard stands on this divisive issue, by and large managed their relationships by agreeing to disagree. But from time to time bitterness would emerge, and the forums for this were both the regular city council and county commission meetings. Like the ancient Greek and Roman public forums from which they derived, these public meetings began to move from being a place for civil debate to a venue for airing personal and group grievances. As is usually the case, the most vocal were also the most hard-headed and illogical.

The Animas–La Plata water project as a public issue migrated from an issue for civil discourse, to disagreement, to a matter where minds hardened. And as animosities grew, hardened minds became hardened hearts. When communities fall out over such matters, antagonisms often last for lifetimes and beyond. Thus, what started out as a fairly modest proposal to develop water for farmers in the area became a larger undertaking with implications for energy development and tourism expansion, then migrated into a debate over winners and losers, and finally became a kind of metaphor for human values. What kind of a community do we want? What kind of a world do we want?

And, as with most undertakings of any consequences, two very distinct points of view emerged. What is enough? Haven't we got a pretty good life here already? Why do we want to jeopardize a kind of community Eden? That's all well and good, others would say, but a lot of us haven't made it yet. Why can't we have the same opportunities as you rich folks? What's wrong with letting this area grow and expand and bring in new money and new people? Isn't that the way to make everybody better off?

During this period, back in the day when Daniel Sheridan was still chairman of the county commission, the Monday and Friday coffee club was not immune.

By and large its regulars, who had distinctive points of view on the matters just like everyone else, kept the discussion on a friendly and even keel. Everyone understood where everyone else stood. But as the controversy intensified, subtle frictions emerged.

Mr. Murphy said, Look, this thing's going to be built. We all ought to figure out how we do it best.

Bill Van Ness laughed. As if we have anything to do with it. The big guys are going to build this thing. And they'll decide who gets what. The way it always happens.

The professor said, What "big guys"?

The big guys, Van Ness said. The government, the bankers, the big shots. They don't give a damn what people like us think.

What about all these meetings the city and the county have had over this? the professor asked. Dan and the other commissioners seem to take the opinions from around here pretty seriously.

Ha, Mr. Murphy snorted. Then what? I think Bill's right. The government and the banks are gonna do whatever they want. That's why I say just build the damn thing and let's get on with it. It's gonna happen anyway. So what's all the fuss about? I'm getting tired of all this political football! That's my opinion.

Sam Maynard had listened to all this. Then he said, You're all forgetting one thing: the Indians. They've got a stake in this. And all that energy they've got can't be developed without water. There are some experts now promoting a coal slurry technology.

What's that? someone asked.

You build a big pipeline, Sam said, holding his arms up to form a four- or five-foot diameter. You mine the coal and crush it. Then you mix it with water—a lot of water—and you pump it down the pipeline to where the power plants are. He pointed westward. Then they drain the water off at the power plant and burn the coal in the boilers. Electricity for Phoenix and Los Angeles.

Wait a minute, Bill Van Ness said. That's our water. What happens to the water?

Sam laughed. Bye, bye. You think those people in the desert are going to send it back to us? He laughed again at the thought.

None of this makes sense, the professor said. My conservation group and a lot of outdoors people and hunters and so forth are going to the town meeting tomorrow night with the senator and tell him to quit financing this project. He needs to hear from the other side, our side.

Why in hell would you do a thing like that? Mr. Murphy said. The thing is confused enough already. You'll just make a lot of the folks around here angry.

Tom, the professor said, people who're against the project are angry too. We think we're not being heard. All these big guys Bill's talking about are being heard. They pay these high-priced lobbyists back in Washington to bang on the doors all the time. And they make big contributions to campaigns. Why can't the rest of us go to a town meeting and speak up? I think this whole thing is nothing but a boondoggle for a bunch of fat cats. I like this place the way it is.

Dan Sheridan walked in as Mr. Murphy said, You see, that's what's wrong. A bunch of greenies show up here and start telling us how to run this town and what we can and can't do. That's what I object to. I care as much about this place as anybody. But I've got a business to run. My hardware store's not going to make it unless we get some more customers. I can't sell hardware to a bunch of river rafters and hippies.

I'm not a hippie, Tom, the professor said.

I didn't say you were, Mr. Murphy said. But a bunch of those people you're taking to the senator's town meeting will be. I guarantee it. And last time I checked they hadn't taken a bath in a while either.

Easy, Sheridan said as he placed his hot coffee on the table.

We're talking about the project, Bill Van Ness said.

So I gather, Sheridan said. What else is there these days?

We'd talk about sports, Sam said, except the Rockies are having a bad season and the Broncos don't look to do much better this fall. Anyway, we shouldn't pollute your coffee with a touchy subject you've got something to do with.

Why not? Sheridan said. Everybody else does. Can't walk down Main without getting stopped by one group or another wanting to shut the project down or start it up.

Mr. Murphy glowered. Well, if the professor here and his greenies keep trying to shut this community down it's going to get pretty nasty.

The professor, normally very placid, pushed his chair back. That's not true and you know it. And calling us a bunch of greenies is kind of demeaning, frankly. Not everyone has to agree with you on everything.

Sheridan held up his hand. Okay, now we're not going to let this thing destroy any friendships. At least not if I have anything to do with it. He gestured for the professor to sit down. Instead Smithson headed for the door.

Sam sighed. I don't like the way this thing is going, he said. Everybody can't get his way here. Either the dam will get built or it won't. Either way somebody's going to be disappointed. What I'm afraid of is that the disappointment will turn to anger instead of being forgotten. That's not a good thing.

Couldn't agree more, Sheridan said.

As they all left, Sheridan stopped Sam Maynard. I think it's time you and I talked to Leonard to see if the Utes might help us solve this.

16.

Twelve years later, the Animas–La Plata continued to occupy a kind of civil war status, and Patrick Carroll went to see Duane Smithson, his former history professor. He had a purpose.

Professor, he said as he settled into the worn chair in his mentor's small office, Mr. Sheridan has to be the key to this whole thing. And you're the one to talk to him about it. Why can't you just talk to him about civic duty like you do in your classes?

He doesn't need any lectures on civic duty, Patrick, the professor said.

All this stuff that happened years ago, Patrick said. It's old. Everyone's forgotten. Now's the time for him to pick up where he left off. When he was driven out.

He wasn't "driven out," Smithson said sharply. He walked away. There's a big difference.

Okay, walked away, the young man said. Anyway, he still has a lot of respect in this town.

That he does, the professor said. But there are still those who think he brought it on himself. Or that he was trying to protect someone—

I know, "someone," Patrick said.

—or that he should have been more careful. And so on and so on. The professor moved from behind his desk to occupy the other worn chair. In any case, Mr. Sheridan wishes to be left alone. Whatever the reason, I'm sure he still feels wounded.

Well, that's the thing, Patrick said. If he came back and settled this war, everyone would really respect him. They'd honor him. Besides, I don't know anyone else who can do it. From all I can tell, people around here are getting angrier and angrier at each other. I hear it all the time. Every time I try to cover a story it's "Animas" this and "Animas" that.

Smithson held up his hand. I know. I know. Even our little coffee group. We've been getting together for years. Mr. Murphy and I used to shout at each other. It may not be a war quite yet, but it's surely a kind of a battle. And it's been going on too long for anyone's good.

That's what I'm trying to say, Patrick said. You're one of the leaders of the opposition. And my father was one of the original creators of the Animas–La Plata. He got the whole thing going years ago when he was a member of Congress. Before he died, he was the biggest cheerleader for it.

After you'd been in my classes for a couple of years, the professor said, I began to wonder whether you were related, so I have to admit I looked it up in your files. You never mentioned it, as I recall.

He was what's usually called a colorful character, Patrick said ruefully. Not always easy to get along with as a father either. But I have to confess that my interest in the history of the Animas–La Plata began over the dinner table when I was a kid. That's all he ever talked about. It was his big purpose in life.

You did write your senior paper on that history, as I recall, the professor said.

Patrick shook his head. I practically had to. He insisted before…before he dropped dead.

In any case, it's hard to spend much time in these parts without being drawn into it one way or the other, Smithson said. I know that from personal experience.

So, that's my idea, Professor, the young man said. In a way I represent, through my father, I guess, one point of view. And, as a big environmentalist, you represent the other.

Not very big, the professor demurred.

Okay, *leading* environmentalist, the former student said. So, here's my idea. The two of us should go to Mr. Sheridan, more or less representing both sides, and propose that he get back involved by becoming the mediator of this whole matter.

Smithson took some time to think. He shook his head sadly. He'll never do it. At least I don't think he will. Who are we? Self-appointed spokesmen for the community? We don't have the power or the authority to even suggest mediation, let alone the mediator. Besides, Mr. Sheridan likes his privacy. He's a friendly man. But he's also a solitary man. He likes it up there where he lives.

Patrick Carroll moved to the edge of the creaking chair. But it's a chance for him to play a role. From all I can tell, everyone had respect for him before all that trouble. You and some others were pushing him for governor. This is his chance to come back.

Smithson smiled. He doesn't want to "come back," as you say. Why? To do what? I can absolutely guarantee you that he doesn't have a politically ambitious bone in his body. It's the last thing in the world he would want to do now.

I'm not necessarily talking about politics, Patrick said. I'm talking about becoming a leading citizen…playing a role…helping solve a big problem, heal a wound.

The professor thought again. That's a little closer to it where Mr. Sheridan's concerned. I've never spoken to him about it, and I never will. But it would be only human for him to want to lay to rest all that speculation from years ago. Smithson was silent again. Then he continued, He cares a lot about this community. He loves Durango. Sheridans have been here almost from the beginning. It's his home. It's where he'll die. It has to grieve him that old friends are becoming enemies.

The young man now nodded vigorously.

Smithson continued. He wouldn't get involved to try to salvage his reputation. Most of us around here don't think he needs to. But if he thought he might prevent a local civil war or keep the place from dividing down the middle, that would be a powerful argument for him.

That's exactly my point, Patrick said. That's it. If he were convinced that he might have some role to play that no one else could play, to settle this thing peacefully, and to everyone's satisfaction—

It's not going to be settled to everyone's satisfaction, the professor interrupted.

—but at least for most people in Durango, the young man continued, then he would at least have to give it some thought.

Smithson smiled. I know the first thing he'll say is, What can I do that anyone else can't do?

Patrick smiled and responded, The tribe. The Southern Utes. That's his unique weapon. Where they are concerned, with the possible exception of Mr. Maynard, he is their most trusted friend. I believe he is the key to the Indians and the Indians are the key to the Animas–La Plata.

17.

On the day years back when Daniel Sheridan resigned from the La Plata County Commission, Caroline had returned to her large house in the foothills west of Durango to find all traces of her husband gone. His closets were cleaned out, down to and including his laundry. His dresser drawers were empty. Her inspection revealed that his revolver, previously hidden in the sock drawer, and his hunting rifle were gone. Virtually every trace of his existence had disappeared.

She noticed with a degree of grim satisfaction that he had taken no books. He had never been much of a reader, and most of the books were hers in any case. And even more important, he had taken none of her paintings. This also did not surprise her, since he had taken little interest in her artistic efforts.

Caroline had gone to the sun porch with a glass of wine. Just as well that their ten-year marriage had yielded no children, she reflected. Her hopes for an intimate, romantic relationship had never really materialized. Their years in New York and then a few years in Denver on the way to Durango had been characterized by his professional preoccupations and her activities in the investment world. They had been social enough everywhere they had lived, though she had become increasingly restless with the frequent parties, charity balls, and evenings out in the cities even as he had been increasingly swept up in them.

Socially, they had evolved into a two-car family by the time they moved to Durango. She left early, and he stayed late. For a while, the independent bank he had acquired in Durango proved satisfying to him, and they adjusted well to the informal small community life. Their friends tended to derive from the professional class of lawyers and doctors. As a leading banker, Russell Chandler quickly became a pillar in the Chamber of Commerce and the service clubs. He also became an officer in the state banking association. Caroline attempted to participate in garden clubs and local charities but within a year or so began to spend most of her time trying to improve her painting skills.

As newcomers they made it a point to attend as many city council and county commission meetings as they could, often accompanying the Farnsworths, who made an effort to introduce them to the Durango area. They became acquainted, through various business and social affairs, with the mayor, the members of the council, and the commissioners and knew most of them on a first-name basis.

Caroline now studied the sun reflecting through the golden wine. She thought of the evening when the chairman of the county commission, Daniel Sheridan, had introduced himself and welcomed them to Durango. That was now three years ago. She had been impressed with his easy manner, his quiet authority and self-possession, and his uncommon aura of remoteness. It wasn't as if he was hiding anything, she thought, his direct green-eyed gaze belied that. It was that he seemed solitary even in the midst of friends and neighbors. In itself, that remoteness had stimulated her interest and curiosity.

She now sighed and found herself amazed not to find her husband's flight more surprising. It was almost as if she had expected it all along, sooner or later. If he was going to leave, and she supposed she had vaguely assumed he might someday, it would be without notice and without discussion or confrontation. That was Russell. A sip of wine later she wondered if she should care where he went. She supposed not. If he wanted her to know, he would find a way to tell her—eventually.

Only after half an hour did she go inside to find the plain manila envelope on the dining room table. She filled her wine glass and took it and the envelope outside once again to the sun porch. It was now late afternoon. He would have known that she would be in the hill country painting most of the day and had planned accordingly.

In the envelope were official documents: the deed to the house; a contract providing for her to receive half the proceeds of the sale of the bank, then nearing completion; and the transfer of a mildly handsome sum to her savings account. Nothing more. No forwarding address. No goodbye. She had to smile. Oh, Russell, you are—were—so predictable.

The money was a help she didn't really need. It was his form of conscience salving. She had maintained her own banking and investment portfolios from the time of their marriage, and he knew her to have more than enough to live on comfortably for the rest of her life.

Only after she began to return the documents to the manila envelope did she find the small white sealed envelope. In it she found this note: "C: You may initiate divorce proceedings on the grounds of abandonment, or whatever. I will not contest it—even to allege adultery. R"

Caroline took matches from the kitchen and returned to the porch with the note. She studied the wine glass, then took a large swallow. She lit a match and burned the note. She swallowed hard and resolved not to cry. Not now, not then. She shook her head. It was all so unfair, so unjust. How had all this happened? Who had introduced this serpent into the Eden of southwestern Colorado? Was it money? Was it power? Was it politics? Or, was it perhaps envy?

Two weeks later the *Durango Herald* had reported the sale of the Chandler bank to a regional banking conglomerate. And some weeks after that, the *Herald* had carried a small notice of the uncontested divorce of Caroline Chandler from Russell Chandler. Caroline would later thank Frances Farnsworth for burying the notice in random news and notes on a back page. By then, in any case, word had circulated that Russell had left, and naturally there was speculation and gossip about the circumstances. For a number of months the community would not see Caroline and Daniel Sheridan in the same location or even the same neighborhood. Time would later ease these restrictions.

Caroline had found it easy to sell the large home in the west suburbs of Durango. She knew exactly where she would relocate and quietly bought the small ranch northwest of town from an elderly couple who themselves were looking to move into town. The house was not large. But it was immaculately maintained and had a small barn for the young mare she acquired at the livestock auction. Best of all, the house had a southwest-facing solarium that she converted into her painting studio. From there she looked out onto a two- or three-acre meadow filled with wild mountain flowers and dotted with pine trees and in which she often saw small deer herds grazing throughout the year.

The place was reasonably secluded, with the house a quarter-mile from the gate and split-rail fencing surrounding most of the ten acres or so, including the horse's grazing area.

Caroline had given thought to leaving Durango and

returning to the city, either back to New York or perhaps the San Francisco Bay Area. She had come to trust Frances Farnsworth about such matters and had organized a lunch with her to discuss it.

You came to the right person, Mrs. Farnsworth said. You know that Murray and I are from New York and we chose to abandon it for this place almost four decades ago. She waved her hand in the direction of the town.

Caroline said, Did you ever regret it?

Never, Mrs. Farnsworth said. Never. They've got the Metropolitan and Madison Avenue and all that. I miss the Metropolitan—though we did get there every couple of years—but I don't miss Madison Avenue and all that stuff. This is real life here. I'm going to sound corny, but this— Durango—is what America was supposed to be.

Caroline shook her head. I haven't lived here nearly as long as you, but I do know what you mean. There isn't the big city excitement, but there is a genuine sense of real life.

Do you miss the city? her older companion asked.

Not really, Caroline said. It helped to spend a few years in Denver...to kind of decompress. But I've come to feel that I belong here. She hesitated, then said, I don't want to be a subject of gossip or laughter around here. My thought about leaving has to do with not wanting to be... some kind of object of discussion.

Mrs. Farnsworth said, Oh, please. People here like you. You must know that. They think you are...classy, I guess...but also a real person. It comes through.

Yes, Caroline said, but now I'm a real divorced person.

My dear, Mrs. Farnsworth said, in the minds of most of the people around here that I know, your stock has gone up. I shouldn't say it, but under the circumstances I will. Your husband was not particularly well liked.

I hope they know that I like it here, that I do feel comfortable here.

I hope you don't mind my saying so, but your husband—your former husband—never felt that way, did he?

Caroline thought and then said, I don't mind, and you're right. He tried to fit in. He even had some political ambition—mayor or congressman or something. But he didn't fit in. When he wore his suits he looked out of place, and when he tried to dress down he looked like some drugstore cowboy.

They both laughed. Then Mrs. Farnsworth said, But you took right to it, didn't you? You felt at home here.

I did, and it was strange, Caroline said, because I've never lived in a small town. But this was like coming home. Russell missed the sirens, but I didn't.

He what? Mrs. Farnsworth asked.

He missed the sirens. He used to wake up in the night and he was almost afraid. It's too quiet, he would say. There has to be some noise out there somewhere. This ungodly quiet is driving me nuts, he'd say.

Mrs. Farnsworth waited, drank her coffee, and then said, But that wasn't all, was it?

Caroline shook her head. No, that wasn't all.

Why did he form this grudge against Dan Sheridan? Mrs. Farnsworth asked. What was that all about? If you don't mind my asking.

I don't mind, Caroline said. It had happened before, after we met and into our marriage. There was a type of man he instinctively didn't like. I've thought about it. It was a type. Mostly men who were self-contained, self-sufficient, who seem as if they could make it even if they were dropped on the moon, or in the desert, or…up in the Weminuche. Dan Sheridan never did a thing to Russell, to my knowledge. He was always polite, always cordial. But Russell quickly came to dislike him—he'd say negative things—and then he couldn't stand him. A couple of times within the last year, Dan would start across the room toward us and Russell just took off. It was embarrassing.

May I tell you something? Mrs. Farnsworth asked.

Of course, Caroline said.

He was jealous of Dan. He thought you would be more attracted to Dan than to him. He envied Dan. He wanted to be like Dan, but he couldn't.

No, Caroline responded, I gave him no reason. I went out of my way not even to talk about Mr. Sheridan when Russell's resentments began to appear.

That's alright, dear, sweet Caroline, Mrs. Farnsworth said. Because he couldn't be like Dan, he took it out on him. Insecure women are all insecure in their own way. Insecure men are all alike.

As they left the small restaurant, Mrs. Farnsworth took Caroline's arm. I hope you'll stay, she said. I think you should stay. I have a sense that—perhaps like me—this is where you belong.

A few days later, Caroline signed the papers for her mountain property, and she moved in shortly thereafter. That was just after the controversy involving Daniel Sheridan.

18.

The Southern Utes, with the actions of Congress and court decisions on resource rights, were on the way in the mid- and late 1990s to the establishment of their resource company Red Willow and were receiving advice on how to manage their new trust fund, whose revenues were beginning to grow. They were being besieged by investment advisors and investment funds, all of whom had elaborate, sometimes baroque, financial systems for maximizing gain. Almost all these schemes were focused on the near term and laid out intricate development plans that, for certain fees, would direct the tribe's newfound wealth into immediate returns for individual tribal members. In every case, the paragraphs regarding fees were near the end of lengthy proposed retainer contracts, and all were in small type.

Leonard Cloud and his tribal council found themselves spending increasing amounts of time with Sam Maynard and his law firm. Having been relative outcasts for well over a century, the Utes now were everyone's new friends, particularly everyone who could smell money. There were enough tribal council members who had been manipulated by one kind of immigrant American or another to make them wary. They trusted Maynard, and they had reason to. He and his partners had always treated them fairly, had never propagated large legal bills, and had shrewdly advised the tribe on a number of occasions of one party or another to steer clear of.

But Cloud and his colleagues were troubled nevertheless. On one occasion in the Maynard law firm, he told Maynard, Every way we look at our development plans, we run up against the water problem. Even though we have the new federal laws about our water rights, having the rights and having the water are two different things.

Sam Maynard nodded. You're right, Mr. Cloud. You've got established rights to the Animas and a lesser amount in the Florida and smaller streams, but it clearly isn't enough to meet the requirements of large-scale mineral development. Some of the proposed technologies are water intensive. Besides, you have downstream obligations to lower basin users in New Mexico to return some of those flows to the stream.

It gets down to the Animas–La Plata, doesn't it? Leonard Cloud said. It always gets down to that project.

Absolutely, Maynard said. If we can't find a way to restart the project, get some federal construction money, and get it going, the Southern Utes are going to hit their heads on a development ceiling. You'll be better off than you were, but not nearly well enough off to create that trust fund for the future that you've decided on.

After the other council member left, Cloud and Maynard walked across the street for coffee. Leonard Cloud was a placid man, measured and thoughtful, not one to become agitated. But his demeanor now was decidedly edgy. Sam, things aren't good around here these days, he said. He waved in the general direction of the town and beyond. It doesn't seem like Durango these days. The atmosphere is not good.

Right enough on that, Leonard, Maynard said. My family's been here well over fifty years and I've never seen this place in such an uproar. The longer this project stays unresolved, the more this community becomes a political war zone. We've got neighbors who've lived next door to each other for decades and now won't speak to each other.

Cloud said, I ran into Sheriff Ramsay the other day. He was making his weekly cruise through the reservation, and he stopped in to our council offices. He was pretty casual about it, but he made it clear that there are one or two hotheads that might want to make trouble. He asked the tribal law enforcement team to be on the lookout.

This isn't like Durango, Sam Maynard said. We've had our politics and our campaigns and our debates about this and that. But we're going to have to either build this project or kill it and move on. Otherwise, it's a sore that could become some kind of cancer pretty quick.

What have you heard from the feds? Cloud asked.

Since you and I were back in Washington a couple of months ago, Maynard said, I've kept in touch with the staffs of our congressmen and senators and, though they're committed to helping us, it's a struggle to get the construction money. All they can talk about back there is balancing the budget.

Cloud said, But they've got to understand this project's important. We can't get anything done without it.

Understood, Maynard said. But you've got five hundred other people in the Congress who've got some federal project they think is as important as ours. I made your point to Senator Thornton's staff guy and he said, Listen, we can get votes for Animas–La Plata, but you know what that means? It means Thornton has to vote for projects in every state those votes come from—and there goes your balanced federal budget.

So what you're saying is, we're stuck, Cloud said. To

get the fed's dollars, our congressional folks have to trade votes, and next election time they get crucified for running up spending.

Sam Maynard nodded. Politically, that's the way it works. But I'll keep in touch with them, and maybe they'll figure something out. In the meantime, though, when any of the congressmen come down here, they get an earful from the project opponents. So they're trapped in the local politics. They support the project and half of southwestern Colorado is angry. They oppose the project and the other half of southwestern Colorado is angry.

That's why we pay them the big bucks, Sam, Cloud said and then laughed wryly.

19.

Mrs. Farnsworth had always had great admiration for Daniel Sheridan but could not claim a close friendship. She had come to believe some years after Sheridan left office that he had been treated unfairly, both by the press and by some elements of the community. As to her own paper, the *Herald,* she and her husband had struggled to treat him fairly during that period when the controversy was treated in the statewide Denver papers as a scandal and a sensation. On more than one occasion, she had gone back through all the *Herald* stories from the time and was struck by a realization. Except for his brief announcement of his resignation—with great regret—from the county commission, Sheridan had never made a comment or submitted to an interview. He had refused to speak in his own defense.

Mrs. Farnsworth spent time considering this. Why had he not? Why not approach the Farnsworths for an open-ended discussion of the matter and get his story on the record? His silence had been assumed, especially in an age of ego and self-advancement, as a tacit admission of guilt—if not of corruption, then of something. Why else would he not speak out and speak up?

Had she known Daniel Sheridan better, she would have sought him out and simply, in her notoriously direct manner, asked him these questions. Give your side of the story, she would have told him. Don't let your accusers dominate the matter. There has to be more to this than what was alleged about taking money from that investment bank to buy favor with the Ute tribal council and, in the process, pay off a blackmailer.

When she thought about it, and she found herself doing so more often now, it frustrated her. She believed in fairness and justice. She and Murray had editorialized against community prejudgment and in favor of under-standing all the facts before rendering opinions. Anyone who knew anything about Daniel Sheridan had to believe that this man was incapable of bribery and intimacy with a prominent woman in the community. But there it was, the allegations were there—though her review of the story caused her to be struck by how much of what was accepted as fact was actually rumor and hearsay—and the only one who knew what really happened would not speak.

During the hell week when everything had come crash-ing down, Caroline Chandler had not been available. A *Herald* reporter had sought her out. She was not at home. She was not painting in the high country. She was not to be found. It was maddening to Sheridan's friends and supporters that neither Sheridan nor Caroline would publicly deny an improper relationship. But, thinking back on it later, Mrs. Farnsworth understood from her years in journalism that a denial is cause for yet another round of stories based on the denial. To deny is to add grist to the rumor and journalism mills.

She wanted to ask Sheridan so many things, and if she knew him better, she would do it. But he was a solitary man and certainly would not welcome a return to that painful era that had changed his life. She wanted to know whether he had urged Caroline to escape, to find refuge with friends on the East or West coast, until the furor abated. Though she was a professional newspaper publisher, she knew that was none of her business, even as many in her industry believed everything was their business.

Mrs. Farnsworth pondered whether Caroline might someday open up to her about the whole matter. Most now assumed that Caroline and Sheridan had an intimate relationship, but no one knew for sure, and by now very few people in Durango and surroundings cared. Times had changed since those days more than twelve years ago, and it was all old news. For herself, Mrs. Farnsworth hoped that they did. She had grown enormously fond of Caroline and considered her almost one of her grown children.

She doubted the opportunity would arise for her ever to know Daniel Sheridan that well. He was just not that kind of man.

Her romantic streak wished them well. They both seemed to her to be high-caliber, quality human beings and, God knows, she thought, there are not enough of them around these days to waste any.

The day finally came sometime later to explore the Sheridan mystery. She passed by Kroeger's Hardware store on 9th Street one Saturday morning and encountered Dan Sheridan coming out carrying a tool box and a coiled length of lariat rope. Good morning, Mr. Sheridan, she said.

How do you do, Mrs. Farnsworth? he responded.

Very well, especially on a day like this. Which way are you headed?

Sheridan nodded to the parking lot a block away. Got to throw this stuff in the pickup, he said.

Mrs. Farnsworth said, I'm going that way and will walk along, unless you object.

No ma'am, he said. No objection at all. A pleasure to see you out and about today. I've been meaning to say, since Murray passed away those months ago, if you ever need anything fixed around your place, I'd be pleased to help out. I'm an amateur repairman, but not a bad one at that.

You're very kind, Mr. Sheridan. My son drops into town every month or so, and he's been very good about fix-up, patch-up. But I greatly appreciate the offer. Now, I assume, given your place way up the Florida Road, that you wouldn't take too kindly to an emergency plumbing crisis in the middle of the night.

This made Sheridan laugh. Well, now, that's a horse of a different color. It's not the middle of the night that would bother me so much, it's that I don't know the first thing about plumbing. When it clogs up at my place, I'm on the phone to Slocomb's right away. But anything else your son can't take care of, don't hesitate to call.

They reached the dusty red pickup and Sheridan

unloaded the lariat rope and tools into the back. He waved to the lady and said, A good day to you, Mrs. Farnsworth.

She hesitated, then on a sudden whim said, Mr. Sheridan, if I were to invite you to dinner some evening, what would you say?

Sheridan looked surprised. Well, I don't know. I guess I'll have to wait until that situation arises. But as a general principle, I make it a practice to respond politely to dinner invitations. There just haven't been that many occasions that have arisen, come to think of it.

Then, I'm inviting you, Mrs. Farnsworth said. Let me look at my calendar and give you a call. You do answer your telephone, don't you?

Sheridan laughed. I do. But it doesn't ring any more often than dinner invitations arise. Surely, just give me a call. My number's not in the book, but I seem to recall that you might have it from times gone by. He suddenly remembered that she had tried to reach him during his troubled times.

I do have it, she said. But if I can't find it, I know who to ask. She started away, then turned back. By the way, you wouldn't mind if I invited someone else—say, Caroline Chandler—to join us.

Sheridan pulled the straw Stetson just slightly lower above his eyebrows and looked at her steadily. Of course, I wouldn't mind, he said. It would be a pleasure to see you both.

Then they parted.

20.

Professor Duane Smithson had given much thought to his former student Patrick Carroll's idea of approaching Daniel Sheridan with the notion of intervening with the Southern Utes to resolve the Animas–La Plata water project and eventually heal the deep divisions in Durango. He cared passionately about the place. He knew its history from the beginning as part of his professional status as the preeminent historian of southwestern Colorado and one of the most highly recognized historians in the state. His books on Colorado history filled more than one library shelf and were notable for the life and energy their author imbued them with.

He himself was not the man, the professor had concluded. He had known Sheridan so long and had been so close to him over the years that he simply could not bring himself to pressure his friend to return to a more or less public role in a highly visible and contentious controversy that was only growing in bitterness and that had so much Sheridan history wrapped up in it. For Sheridan to insert himself into the Animas–La Plata dispute, even at the urging of well-meaning, community-concerned people, would be the equivalent of sending a badly wounded veteran back into the conflict where he had received his wounds.

Yet, Smithson thought, who else? When you looked at all the players, positions had been taken and sides had hardened. There was virtually no one left who both understood the conflict and possessed the wisdom to intervene. Beyond wisdom, Smithson said to himself, Sheridan has a kind of moral authority on his side. Smithson could not help but smile at the idea. After fifteen years, was he the only one in this whole corner of the state who thought Daniel Sheridan had moral authority? Better not use that phrase with anyone else he talked to. Most of them would think he was crazy.

No, he had no illusions. If Dan Sheridan could be persuaded to find a way to bring the Indians into the equation, it presented a chance to resolve the matter once and for all. But it would have to be done quietly, without notice or fanfare. Sheridan wouldn't have it any other way in any case.

The most powerful instrument Sheridan possessed was the trust the Southern Utes had in him. Smithson knew this from his study of early and more recent Ute history. The Sheridan family had been among the first to quietly embrace the tribe and build friendships with its members. Sheridan's father and grandfather between them had known every tribal chairman reaching back well over half a century. The stories of money lent, houses built, classes taught, and medicine provided by the Sheridans would never completely be told. And Daniel Sheridan would be the first to discourage its telling. But that history represented a priceless storehouse of trust no one else in the region possessed.

Sheridan was the man to bring the Utes into the project on a full-partner basis and heal the wounds in Durango. It is his duty, the professor thought. It is his burden. But it might also be his destiny. The professor's mind was calibrated to think in those grand terms. His search of human history was intensely focused on the pivotal figure, the actor whose decisions redirected the course of human events. Such figures, in Smithson's mind, were men and women of destiny.

But Duane Smithson was not the man to persuade Daniel Sheridan. Someone else would have to play that role. Ruminating in his cramped office on the Fort Lewis College campus, he suddenly had a bold—beyond bold, shocking— thought. Patrick Carroll, whose idea this was, surely had a role to play. His father, the congressman, had been among the first to seek funding for the Bureau of Reclamation to study a major water storage project on the Animas River. Among those who had held out hope of the project as representing the future of La Plata County and southwestern Colorado, Congressman Carroll was an icon, a godfather of sorts. So his heir must be his successor. But that heir must have the guidance of a more senior figure, a major presence in the drama. It might even be someone who had competed with and even antagonized Sheridan in the bad days.

At first, the professor resisted the idea forming in his mind. It was too far out. It was too illogical. But now he remembered a conversation he had had with Walter Hurley some months ago, quite by accident. Smithson had completed his annual talk to the Durango Rotary Club on strange incidents in Colorado history and old man Hurley had approached him afterward.

Professor, he had said, that was a great talk. Great talk as always. I can't tell you how much I look forward to hearing you every year. Something new and amazing every time. I can't imagine where you unearth those long-ago incidents. But they are truly wonderful.

Smithson said, Thank you very much, Mayor. Walter Hurley was known as Mayor to one and all, though his two terms had ended years ago. He maintained himself as a kind of mayor emeritus.

The mayor had then said a strange and provocative thing. He said, I've been thinking about your old friend Dan Sheridan recently. How's he doing?

The professor was tongue-tied. Mayor Walter Hurley had been the first visible public figure to call for Sheridan to step down from the county commission during the vivid controversy years before. In doing so, he had legitimized the opposition to Sheridan and became its unofficial spokesman. Hurley had intended to quiet the controversy. Instead he fanned it into a raging fire. He had never been known for finesse or cleverness. He was notoriously a blunt instrument. From the public's perspective, he was the first to throw Daniel Sheridan overboard and to send him into his decade-and-a-half exile.

A few days after running into the retired mayor, Professor Smithson called him to ask if he could drop by his home for a few minutes.

Mayor, he said when they met, I have an idea I'd like for you to consider. He then outlined his plan to have the mayor and the son of his old friend Congressman Carroll approach Dan Sheridan and ask him to employ the powerful instrument of his goodwill with the Southern Utes to resolve the Animas–La Plata water project and restore peace to southwestern Colorado.

The aging politician was stunned. Professor, there's nothing I'd rather do than get this water controversy behind us. Lord knows, it's been a cross I've carried almost my whole adult life. And believe me, I'm as concerned as anyone around here about the uproar going on in this town and this county. I've lived here all my life and I've never seen anything like it.

He shook his head and continued. But you and I both know that Mr. Sheridan and I have had our differences all these years. And I don't think there's a chance in the world he's going to let me darken his doorstep, let alone persuade him to get back into this battle.

Smithson said, Do you accept the fact that the Southern Utes are the key to this maze?

Of course they are, Hurley said. If you've thought about this as much as I have, you can't come to any other conclusion.

Smithson said, Do you dispute the fact that Dan Sheridan has a particular, even unique, relationship with Leonard Cloud and the tribe?

Hurley thought awhile and then said, No, as a matter of fact I don't dispute that. I hadn't thought about it, but now that I do I believe you are exactly right. But having accepted all that doesn't lead me to believe that I'm the one who's going to convince him to rejoin the fight. 'Specially after all that history.

How bad do you want to resolve this dispute, Mayor? Smithson asked.

It'd be the best thing I ever did for this community, the old man said. Of course I want it more than anything else. Pat Carroll Senior and I put our whole life into it. Now he's not around to get it finished.

But his son is, the professor said, and you are. And between the two of you I think you can bring Mr. Sheridan back and get him to convince the Indians to accept a position that will end this war.

Mayor Hurley silently considered this at length. You know what you're asking me to do, don't you? he presently said. You're asking me to go hat in hand to Mr. Sheridan and apologize for what I did back then. After a moment, he said, I'm not sure I can do that.

How do you feel about all that business now? Smithson asked.

I feel pretty bad about it. In fact, I feel goddamn bad about it. He didn't understand what I was trying to do, and everybody else thought I had come down on him and driven him out. I just thought he would be a distraction at a critical time to the project and would confuse things even further.

And..., the professor asked.

And...I screwed up. I was wrong. I've always been kinda tone deaf where human feelings are concerned. Just ask the late Mrs. Hurley...if you could. She would have been the first to tell you. No, I played into the hands of the yahoos and sent a good man—a very good man—off into the wilderness, almost literally. I'm damned ashamed of it.

Well, Professor Smithson said, I think it's come time to go back where we started and fix things up.

21.

Tribal chairman Leonard Cloud and two of his trusted tribal council members routinely toured the area up and down the Animas River as it transited the reservation on its way south to New Mexico. Occasionally, they would do the same thing with the Florida and other streams, many dry as dust by the end of summer, after the spring melts and runoffs from the high country. It was a ritual that was born of practicality, checking stream flows and considering how augmented river capacity might be used to fulfill their plans for their people. But it was also a means of connecting and reconnecting with the lifeblood of maternal earth from whom all other natural blessings flowed.

Long before the early immigrant Americans, and even earlier than the Spanish before them, these roaming people of the West had a spiritual connection to water. Of necessity, their encampments were always on or near rivers and streams or the occasional natural pond backed up behind a beaver dam. What had been a matter of practicality for more generations than any Ute could remember had naturally become a matter of religious conviction. Without water there was no life. Water was a gift. Water was life. Water and existence could not be separated. Water itself had a spirit.

When the immigrants came west and settled and built their sod houses, then their outposts, then their villages, then their towns, they depended on water just as much for their livelihood. But they treated it as a commodity, something to be acquired, a subject of capture, then of ownership, trading, and manipulation. They fought over it and more than a few times killed each other over it. This behavior gave rise to the saying known to all ranchers in the West: "Whiskey is for drinkin'; water is for fightin'."

The indigenous people were amazed by this. In the days before the immigrants, no tribe sought to own the water. It was a gift from the Spirit to all humankind. Tribes might fight over herds of buffalo or grazing space or dominion of one kind or another. But rarely over water. Before the machines and the cities came, there was more than enough water for all.

So the Utes watched as the immigrant people, the Americans, settled and were forced to enact laws to parcel out the water of the Animas and other rivers. Commodities had to be regulated and rules were required to determine who got what. You couldn't move around in this new civilization without first establishing a complex body of laws, if for no other reason than to prevent competing claims from being resolved with the Colt and the Winchester. So the lifeblood of the natives, at the spiritual center of their existence, became a commercial commodity to their successors on the land.

The Utes might be confined for their homes and their livelihood to the arbitrary boundaries of a reservation. But that did not also require them to adopt the transformation of an object of reverence into a matter of business and politics.

Leonard Cloud and his brothers parked their trucks near a juniper grove on the Animas and sat in the shade of the trees near the flowing stream. Now, well into the summer, the flow was substantially diminished. The spring snowmelt up in the San Juan Mountains had come and gone. But residential and commercial demands on the river, from Durango and above, continued throughout the year. The Utes got whatever happened to be left.

They picked this place to consider their situation, both because it was familiar and had been used for this purpose before and because they knew also who might be there.

Brother Two Hawks, Cloud said to the older man resting against the juniper trunk, will you be disturbed if we spend a minute or two here?

The old man shook his head. This river is not mine, he said.

Well, then, one of the councilmen said, help us think what we should do about this. Up in Durango they're making big decisions. One way or the other, it comes down on us. They're either going to keep things as they are, which means more people using less water, or they're going to put a dam across the river and store up more water and find more uses for it. If things stay as they are, he said, pointing at the diminished river, here's what we've got. If they build a big reservoir up there, there could be more for us.

Two Hawks had been looking steadily downstream. Those folks, he said presently, are going to do what they are going to do. There is little we can do about it.

The younger council member spoke up. But Father, that's the old way of thinking. We now have this energy here on the res. We finally got the government to recognize that it belongs to us. It changes everything. It means we have power. And when you have power, people have to pay attention. In the old days, we let them run our lives. No more.

Well, I hope you're right, the aged man said. But the power you talk about can work in all kinds of different ways. That snake over there—they stared across the stream and could barely make out the sunning rattler the old man saw clearly—he will not bother you until you try to have power over him.

Leonard Cloud said, Up in Durango, there are a few crazy people who are putting rifles in the gun racks in their pickups. There are all kinds of splits opening up about this water project. And whichever way it goes—this water war—the Ute people, our people, are going to be affected.

We're trying to decide whether we ought to stay well out of it, or whether we ought to get involved to try to settle it.

Two Hawks studied him, then looked downstream again. It is pretty funny, isn't it, when you think about our situation? Who would have thought even a few years ago that anybody up there cared about us one way or the other?

One of the councilmen said, They're even paying attention back there in Washington. The "Great Father"—his tone was derisive—remembered all of a sudden that there were some Indians sitting downstream who might have something to say about all this. What a wonder.

A wonder indeed, Two Hawks said with a smile. I guess our time had to come sooner or later.

Well, it still leaves the question about what we ought to do, Leonard Cloud sighed. Let us know if you have notions to help us. Whatever we do, even if we do nothing, it's going to affect us pretty powerfully. We can't let our people be hurt by this business.

Two Hawks said, Our people have been hurt by much. Yet we survive. We go on. It is in our nature. We were not put here for nothing. I cannot speak for the others, he said, gesturing north toward Durango, but I believe and the old holy men a long time ago believed we didn't just happen to be here. Time goes on and the people up there—again to Durango with a wave—have their own purposes. They will determine their own destiny. We must determine ours. He paused for reflection, then he continued. Though I don't have the TV and all that, I have been following this thing. I listen to what people say. Sometimes I even go up to the town and sit on one of those benches on the street. He laughed. Those tourist people take my picture. It is my service to those people up there. But I also listen to what people say.

He was silent again. Then he said, It's interesting what you can learn by listening. What I learn is what you say. There is bad feeling up there. These people are fighting each other. This is very bad for them. It is very bad for us. So maybe you are right. Maybe we have no choice but to come into this thing. To take a stand. But it must be a stand that represents what is best for our people. And it must be a stand based upon the principles of our people and all people.

After more silence, Leonard Cloud said, Speak about this some more.

Two Hawks said, These people up there invited this struggle, this conflict, when they treated this gift—he pointed at the river—as a business, some kind of legal business. That's done. That's their way. Nothing we can do about that now. But maybe if we get involved in this dispute, maybe we can do some good. Maybe we can point out that this water isn't something you own, something you possess. It is not our way. Maybe we can say, Listen, we don't "own" this river. We share this river. We must honor this water. We must be thankful for it. To fight over this water is to dishonor it. Fighting over this gift of the mother is to dishonor the mother. The others up there may do that. We, the Ute people, cannot do this. It is not in our nature.

The men were silent. Their respect for their elder had grown. They had been reminded what made them different from the modern people. They even thought that circumstances might have given them a destiny.

22.

At his ten-year-old computer in his cubicle at the *Durango Herald*, Patrick Carroll stared at the words from fifteen-year-old stories yet again. This was the second, in some cases the third, time he had done so. Yet even so he could not make sense of it all.

The controversy began with the eighth paragraph in an otherwise routine La Plata County Commission story on page five of the paper. An unidentified citizen angrily denounced the chairman, Dan Sheridan, for improper actions relating to the Animas–La Plata water project and insisted that he reveal the full details of his "sordid" involvement. Nothing more. There was no report on the reaction of other commission members or the audience.

Then, a week or so later, there was a letter to the editor from someone not readily recognizable in the community calling for Sheridan's resignation on the grounds that he was manipulating the project for his own benefit. Though this kind of activity wasn't common, most of Durango paid little attention on the assumption these people were unrelated public scolds of the kind that randomly appear. Then, after Sheridan gave a report on the issues confronting the county at a local service club, a local businesswoman, new to the community, rose to confront him with these accusations and insisted on his response.

Daniel Sheridan had seemed awkward and even somewhat defensive, at least in the *Herald*'s report of the exchange, and brushed the question aside with the comment that his only interest in Animas–La Plata was what was best for the region.

Patrick Carroll found a story in the *Durango Herald* morgue of a more serious incident about two weeks after the confrontation at the meeting. At a public town hall meeting conducted by his father, Congressman Patrick Carroll, at least two people stood up to denounce Sheridan and call for both his resignation and a thorough investigation of his involvement in Animas–La Plata. Each claimed to have evidence that Sheridan was pursuing his own financial interests in the project and that he might be guilty of unethical or even illegal practices.

Caught off guard, the congressman said that he had known the Sheridan family for many years, that he had never known of anyone in the family, including Dan Sheridan, to be engaged in anything like what was being alleged, and concluded by insisting that the accusers produce whatever evidence they had. The two accusers stormed out of the meeting, shouting as they left that the congressman was merely covering up for his crony friend and that it proved all politicians were alike.

All this activity covering a month or so seemed unrelated. But then, after a monthly meeting of the county commission, one of Daniel Sheridan's co-commissioners told a *Herald* reporter, in answer to her persistent questions, that perhaps Sheridan ought to disclose any private interest he might have in the project. When pressed by the reporter as to whether this ought to be a matter for the commission itself to investigate, the confused commissioner allowed that any public body like the county commission had to keep its own house in order to belay any citizen doubts.

That comment produced a page two story in the *Herald* the following day headlined: "Commissioner Calls for Full

Sheridan Investigation." The next day, a *Rocky Mountain News* stringer from Grand Junction appeared in Durango to probe what seemed like a promising public scandal. That reporter tracked down the two protestors at the congressman's town hall meeting and quoted both in the *News* as saying they had solid evidence, though no documents, that Sheridan was receiving payoffs from a prominent New York investment bank for intervening with the Southern Ute Tribe on behalf of the bank. They further alleged that Sheridan might need the money also to help cover up a scandalous relationship with a prominent local woman.

Now the Sheridan story was statewide and was attracting attention in business, social, and political circles in the region. Though noted for their western laissez-faire attitudes toward personal privacy, even the worthy citizens of Durango proved not to be immune to interesting, if not also salacious, gossip. The Sheridan story was spreading and increasing in intensity and dimension.

Patrick Carroll tried to take an objective approach to it. But as he had earlier told Professor Smithson and even Mr. Sheridan himself, it still didn't make sense. Who were the early questioners? Why weren't they identified? Why hadn't the *Herald* insisted on identifying them and questioning them before running the story? He knew the answer to the last question at least. The reporter would have had to spend a day, or several, finding those making the accusations and persuading them to identify themselves and to document their charges, and then the story would be several days old.

Sheridan could certainly have done better at explaining himself once confronted at the service club lunch. But how? How do you disprove a negative? Once charged, a public official has the burden of disproving something that didn't happen. The simple denial, based primarily on reputation and standing, becomes just that. And a denial is a story, Patrick Carroll ruefully thought.

It was at this point that the former mayor, Walter Hurley, had intervened with his public call, contained in yet another letter to the *Durango Herald* editor, for Daniel Sheridan to take a leave of absence or even resign until the whole thing got cleared up. This would be best, he argued, for Mr. Sheridan, but it would also be in the best interest of the community. Starting with an anonymous rumor, then accusation, the weight of the furor had now shifted solidly against Daniel Sheridan. At the monthly meeting of the county commission a week or so later, the vice chair of the commission read the one-sentence letter from Daniel Sheridan resigning, "with great regret," from the commission.

By now Patrick Carroll was making himself a pest with his boss, Mrs. Farnsworth. He had worn out his welcome with the *Herald*'s managing editor, who constantly pushed him to leave the ancient story alone and get on with current issues and who, in any case, had not been around when the Sheridan case had erupted and had no interest in it or time for it. But the young reporter knew that Mrs. Farnsworth had had a ringside seat at the ruckus those many years ago and that she had hinted in the past that she was less than pleased with its handling at the time by the community at large and by her paper.

He did deny it, she said with a sigh to the rumpled young reporter leaning against her doorframe yet again. And, guess what, we ran the denial. "Sheridan Denies Accusations." What else could we do? But I think that was the turning point for him. I don't know for sure, but my instincts tell me that's when he saw no way out. Charge. Counter-charge. Accusation. Denial.

He should have fought it, Patrick said with heat. He shouldn't have just folded and walked away. He wasn't guilty of anything. But he left it hanging in the air. And there it's been all these years. He shouldn't have let them get away with it.

Sit down, Mrs. Farnsworth said. She looked out of the window toward the San Juans looming to the northeast. She turned a penetrating gaze on the young man. I'm about to give you a life lesson, she said, and I want you to listen. People of honor do not need to "fight." To descend into the muck that now underlies much of public life is to lose your self-respect. And when you've lost that, you've lost everything. There is something much more important than being chairman of the La Plata County Commission. There is something much more important than being governor of this state. There is even something more important that being president of the United States. That something is dignity. It is personal honor. It is self-respect. And without those things, none of us is worth anything.

Patrick was subdued. She let him ponder this. Then she said, Daniel Sheridan is an honorable man. That means he deserves respect. He has earned it. He has earned it as much by how he has lived his life since this disaster as he did before it. He didn't have to justify himself to anyone. To fight, as you say, for your dignity is to admit that someone else has the power to take it away. They don't. No one does. No one can take away your dignity. You may surrender it. But you do that by patterns of behavior, by being corrupt and corrupted, by lack of character. Except for my late husband, I believe Daniel Sheridan is the most honorable man I have ever met. His character may be assaulted, and it surely was. But his character is strong, it is solid, and, by any human measure, it is beyond reproach.

The young man considered this. Then he said, I intend to write this. That's what I'm trying to do, to write what you just said.

Don't, she said. I've already told you, this paper will not run it. I'm sad to say this, but journalism isn't in the business of character rehabilitation. We report the news. And what I've just told you isn't news to the large majority of people in Durango. Besides, we can't go back and make things right. What would we do? Run an editorial endorsing Daniel Sheridan for county commissioner? It would be a joke. We can't go back and fix things. You can't, and I can't. And, most of all, Daniel Sheridan would hate it.

23.

Not too long after this exchange with Patrick, Mrs. Farnsworth hosted dinner for Caroline and Sheridan. Her large, comfortable house, which she had occupied with her late husband, sat in the foothills on the outskirts of Durango to the west. It was not too far from the house Caroline and her former husband had bought when they moved to Durango years earlier. Caroline had been there before, but Sheridan had not.

They arrived separately. Sheridan handed the hostess a bunch of wildflowers he had picked late that afternoon in his high meadow.

After placing the flowers in a small vase on the dining room table, Mrs. Farnsworth served them drinks on her side porch facing the distant San Juans. I hope you understand that I'm not wearing my publisher's hat this evening, she said.

Caroline laughed and Sheridan said, Yes, ma'am. Thank you.

There is no agenda, Mrs. Farnsworth said in her straightforward manner. I've just not had a lot of company recently, and you two came to mind. She turned to Sheridan and said, Actually, I had invited Caroline for this evening when I ran across you at Kroeger's Hardware a few days ago. So I thought, why not. It's no secret you two know each other.

We do, indeed, Caroline answered. Aside from being ranch people, more or less—he's a real rancher and I pretend to be—we are also hobbyists of sorts. I pretend to paint and he actually carves.

Really, Mrs. Farnsworth said to Sheridan. Carves what, may I ask?

Chunks of wood, Mrs. Farnsworth, he replied. Just plain old chunks of wood. Mostly walnut, which is great carving wood for an amateur like me. It's soft and kind of buttery, I guess you'd say. Some occasional mahogany, more for its color than its texture. It's more brittle and harder to manage. I tried some of the native wood some years back. But not very much of it lends itself to carving.

Mrs. Farnsworth asked whether his pieces were for sale, and he laughed. Oh, no ma'am. They're pretty primitive. Figures and such. Some Indian, some just natural creatures.

GARY HART

Caroline said, Don't listen to him. I have one or two of his "figures" and they're beautiful. Primitive, yes. But strikingly symbolic, many of them.

Mrs. Farnsworth said she had an interest in such things and hoped to see some of his work someday.

Throughout the cocktail hour their discussion ranged through a variety of local matters and dismaying troubles on the national and world scenes. Despite her efforts to engage Sheridan at length, he largely responded to her topics with questions of his own, asking first her, then Caroline, their respective opinions on this or that. It was only after the end of the evening that Mrs. Farnsworth realized how little he had actually said, though he seemed at the time to be fully engaged in the discussion. She noted with admiration his ability to be fully part of the conversation without revealing many opinions of his own. This, she reflected, was particularly true of the political issues of the day.

After drinks they filled their plates in the kitchen and moved into the dining room, with Mrs. Farnsworth at the head of a long formal table and Caroline and Sheridan facing each other. Sheridan uncorked a bottle of pinot grigio with an expensive-looking Italian label that Caroline had brought, and he filled their glasses.

Mr. Sheridan, Mrs. Farnsworth began.

Dan, please, Mrs. Farnsworth.

Alright then, Frances for me. I want your opinion on the Animas–La Plata these days. You haven't been visible on this in many years, but you understand the project top to bottom, and it's stuck. It's in the ditch, and it must be got out or we're going to have a civil war around here. I for one intend for that not to happen. So under these circumstances, it would be a waste not to have your opinion, if not also your advice.

Well, Frances, he said, though my hide is as tough as any one of my steers, this is a topic that I've left alone for quite a while and I'd just as soon leave it alone, if you don't mind.

I do mind, Mrs. Farnsworth said vigorously. This is your community just as much as it is ours—she pointed at Caroline and herself—and you're darn well responsible as we all are to see it doesn't end in some kind of shoot-out disaster. It's simply unconscionable what's going on around here, especially among supposedly civilized people.

Taken aback by her directness, her challenge, Sheridan tried to regroup. I didn't say I wasn't concerned. What I meant to say is that there are a still a good number of people in these parts who'd not welcome me into this debate.

I'm not asking you to get into the debate, Daniel, I'm asking you simply to tell me what, in your judgment, ought to be done.

Sheridan took his time refilling the wine glasses while Caroline went for a second bottle. Alright, he said, here's the only way this thing is going to end up without a canyon down the middle of Main Avenue for the next fifty years. The Southern Utes get their fair share of the water from the project—in perpetuity, not for a few years—so that they can carry out their energy projects and build decent communities on that reservation and set up their long-range trust fund. Then they sign off on the project and Leonard Cloud and Sammy Maynard go back to Washington and tell the government that this is the deal. And this deal, with the Utes as full partners and major beneficiaries, is the only way there will ever be an Animas–La Plata storage dam and distribution system. Full stop.

Caroline nodded in agreement. Leonard Cloud told me the very same thing, she said.

You've talked to Mr. Cloud? Mrs. Farnsworth said with a degree of astonishment.

Of course, Frances. Why not? He's a thoughtful man.

I know he's a thoughtful man, Mrs. Farnsworth said. But I didn't know you knew him that well.

It all began two or three years ago when all this energy and mineral wealth began to come together, the younger woman said. He contacted me, said he knew I had financial experience, and wanted my ideas.

Well, now, the older woman said. Isn't that something. Good for you. I had no idea. What did you tell him?

Caroline smiled. I thought you were not a journalist tonight, Frances. I'm not a paid consultant, so I have no contractual restrictions. But I know you'll understand the confidentiality of my advice. I simply helped him develop this idea of a long-range trust fund for the tribe's future. He hadn't thought of that and wasn't sure how it might work. Then we took it to the Maynard law firm and they began to reduce it to legal documents and research the tax implications.

Isn't that something, Mrs. Farnsworth marveled again. How in the world did I manage to corral the two smartest people in Durango for dinner at my table to discuss the biggest problem this town has faced in decades, if not ever?

Now Caroline and Sheridan laughed together. Only his napkin kept Sheridan from spewing wine across the table. Caroline said, Frances, don't treat us like your reporters. You're pretty transparent, even if you don't think so.

I've gotten to know you well enough to know you carry a whole deck of cards up your sleeve at any given moment.

Mrs. Farnsworth said, Well, I must tell the truth, I actually intended to chalk this evening up to matchmaking. But something tells me I may be a little late for that.

24.

Sam Maynard passed the coffee pot around and said, I'm not going to talk about the tribe's business—won't do it— but I can say what's pretty obvious: Mr. Cloud and the Southern Utes are going to get a fair share of Animas water or there's not going to be a project.

Mr. Murphy said, Hell, every time you turn around these days, they want something else.

Now, Tom, the professor said, you know that's not right. You know their history as well as I do. Everyone around here who can read knows that they've been sitting down there on that reservation for well over a century with almost nothing.

They could have worked and earned more, just like all the rest of us, Mr. Murphy said.

Let's not get into that yet again, Sam Maynard said. We've been over all that. They got some of the worst land in the state of Colorado—probably in the United States for that matter—and they've scratched out a living, barely a living, all these years. They've done their best to get tourism down there, even at the cost of demeaning themselves and dressing up like some damn Hollywood Indians for the

picture-taking. And we—he gestured around the table—
let them have whatever's left over up here, including water.

Bill Van Ness said, You walk out there on Main and
most people would say they just get drunk all the time.
Well, I'll tell you something, if I lived on the res I'd probably drink a little myself.

Mr. Murphy said, I still don't know why they have to get
storage water from the Animas–La Plata. That's our water.

Sam said, Tom, the water belongs to whoever the law
says it belongs to. Now, I encourage you not to push your
argument too far, because Colorado law has said from the
beginning that water from our rivers and streams belongs
to whoever appropriated it first. I don't think there's much
doubt that the Utes appropriated it long before us immigrants showed up here.

Mr. Murphy said, You lawyers and your fancy tricks.
I'm no lawyer, but I know enough to know that "appropriate" means put to beneficial use. Some squaw woman pulling a gourd full of water out to cook with, or washing her
kids in that stream, or a guy letting his horse have a drink
doesn't count as "appropriation."

Right you are, Mr. Murphy, Sam said. Move to the
head of the law class. But there are two things that trump
Colorado law, especially on interstate rivers, which most of
ours are. One is called the Congress of the United States
and the other is called the Supreme Court. They seem to
think the Indians are entitled to a share of water the federal
government pays to dam up.

Well, I'll tell you something, Mr. Murphy said. There's
a whole lot of folks around here who think both of those
outfits are operating way beyond their authority. A lot of us

are ready to throw out the whole kit and caboodle of those people in Washington and start all over again. And we ought to also get a president who's going to put some conservatives on the Supreme Court. I don't know who those people are saying we got to give our water to the Indians.

Sam shook his head and smiled. Mr. Murphy, as Mr. Dooley said, the judges follow the election returns. My bleeding heart is with the Utes and I'm going to see they get a share of water from any project that's built.

Be honest now, Sam, Mr. Murphy grumbled, it's not your heart that's with the Indians. It's your wallet.

Be careful there, Mr. Murphy, Bill Van Ness said. You're walking pretty near the edge.

The professor said, Sooner or later, and it better be sooner, a decision has to be made about the Animas–La Plata or there are not going to be any Monday and Friday coffee clubs around here…and there may not be a Durango left worth living in.

PART TWO

25.

The Weminuche Wilderness Area, created by Congress in 1975, contains upwards of 480,000 acres. It has scores of peaks over 13,000 feet and three Fourteeners located in the granite Needle Mountains toward the western end of the wilderness. Volcanic eruptions millions of years ago threw up the soaring, rugged peaks, and then the glaciers came in several ages to leave behind more than sixty pristine high mountain lakes.

Eighty miles or so of trails follow the Continental Divide to form the spine of the Weminuche and the backbone of America.

The snows that collect in this dramatic high country form the headwaters of dozens of major rivers, primarily the Rio Grande and San Juan Rivers, and many smaller streams, including the Florida River arising a few miles above the Sheridan ranch site.

Over toward the western end of the Weminuche Wilderness are the Needles. And within its ragged high peaks and precarious cliffs arise the streams that feed into the Animas River, called by the Spanish *Rios de las Animas Perdidos*, the river of the lost souls. The area was also notable for its number of lost mines—gold and silver—discovered, traded in a poker game, locations lost in bottles of whiskey, mostly just disappeared. But they were out there, a bonanza if you could just find those lost diggings.

More than once, Daniel Sheridan's place had been the collection point for US Forest Service rangers and expert wilderness rescue teams setting off to pluck unwitting hikers and campers out of the southwestern areas of the wilderness area, stranded there from weather, misread compasses, or dumb fool behavior. You could give these people every kind of instruction on wilderness trekking and what to do, and even more what not to do—and the USFS rangers did their utmost to do so—and they would still run amok.

Sheridan knew the crews, and they all knew him. He was a fixture whenever rescue operations had to be undertaken. It was believed that he knew his southwest quarter of the Weminuche better than anyone, or at least better than anyone since the Ute tribes roamed the area and gave it its name. He had gone through a number of trail horses in his lifetime, mostly Tennessee Walkers with their incredibly sure footing on the loose high mountainous trails, but none had proved as steady, as downright reliable as Red, his current favorite. Red actually seemed to enjoy the treacherous cliffside hanging trails that dropped off to a sure death six or seven hundred feet, or more, below.

On the occasions when Sheridan took Caroline with him up to his hidden lake hideout, he took along a sturdy pack animal with panniers loaded down with a tent, sleeping bags, cooking gear, fishing rods and reels, a whiskey bottle and some good wine, and cornmeal in which to fry the trout.

A few years back, when he first invited her to join him, she was uncertain.

I've spent plenty of time outdoors and on horseback, she had told him, but I've never had to deal with the kind of trails you're talking about.

Nothing to worry about, Sheridan had assured her. That horse I helped you pick out last year, she's trail savvy. I made sure about that. As the old-timers used to say, "The horse knows the way."

What if I get scared going up there—or coming back down? she said.

They had been sitting on old wooden outdoor chairs on the banks of the Florida on his property. Well, now, he looked at her over his whiskey glass, if that were to happen I'd give you a choice. You could just stay right there on the trail. And I suppose sooner or later, probably sooner, one of those old cougars up there would decide you and that filly looked pretty tasty. Or, you could just close your eyes and follow Red and me till we got somewhere without a long drop-off.

She smiled grimly at him and hoped he didn't see her involuntary shiver. What a gentlemanly choice, she said. If you're serious about me coming along to your place up there in the wilderness, I guess I'll either have to learn to trust you and my horse, or I'll have to learn how to fight cougars.

After more than four hours of steady climb on that first occasion, they came around a sharp hairpin turn on the narrow trail, and there was Sheridan's hidden lake. She could not breathe as she took in its beauty. He helped her from her horse and noticed her brush tears from her cheeks.

After a few minutes, while he staked out the riding horses and the pack horse, she said, It is absolutely stunning. It is hard to imagine that there is any place like this on earth. I am speechless.

That's good, Sheridan said. These trees and rocks and those fish in that lake aren't very much used to human talking, surely not from me, so they won't mind it if you don't give them any speeches.

Repeating a familiar process, Sheridan unpacked the panniers, set up the tent, and began to scour the area for firewood. She soon joined him, and together they gathered dry twigs and branches. But Sheridan set out into the trees for heavier wood for the following two or three nights.

Caroline watched him retreat. Then, in a spontaneous move that shocked even her, she pulled off all her sweat-stained trail clothes and ran to the water's edge. She knew she would never have the courage if she entered slowly, so she held her breath and jumped as far out as she could. Though warmed by days of sunlight, the lake water nevertheless was still nothing but melted snow.

Inadvertently and without restraint, after a moment of shock she let out a howl. Immediately, Sheridan dashed out of the tree line toward the lake, dropping firewood as he ran. He was almost at the edge of the lake when he saw her head bobbing ten feet offshore.

How about that, he exclaimed. Now, how about that.

You've got to go back into the trees, she said through chattering teeth. Please, just go back into the trees.

I couldn't do such a thing, ma'am. What if you were to drown? I'd never forgive myself. Plus, I've got all this food and spirits here and I couldn't possibly handle it all myself.

Please, she said, please go back in the trees—or at least just turn your back.

Well, Sheridan said, I guess I could do that. But then what're you going to do? You've still got to get some clothes or something to put on. Look here, he said. Right over there is a towel I brought for you. I'll just go get that and you can get out of that water and dry off while I'm getting a fire going so you don't catch something.

Okay, she chattered.

Besides, he said as he dug a towel out of the pannier, you don't want one of those water finortens to get you.

She shouted, What? A what? What's a "finorten"?

He came back with the towel, turned around, and held the towel behind him. Oh, nothing very much. But they can grow kinda big up here and their teeth do get kinda sharp.

He heard her scrambling out of the water, splashing and gasping as she grabbed the towel held behind his back.

My God, she said. I had no idea. A what? A "finorten"? I never heard of such a thing. What do they do?

Toes, he said, mostly. There are lots of folks down in town and quite a few of these big city camper types that have lost toes. They're just too ashamed to talk about it. But your finortens do go for the toes, mostly.

He started to turn and she said, Wait a minute. I'm not dry yet.

Sheridan looked down at her feet and said, Lucky you. You kept all those toes.

Caroline said, Could you just wait until I get dried off?

Sheridan said, I don't mean to shock you or anything. But I saw a naked lady once before.

26.

For almost two months, since he began the research for his Daniel Sheridan profile, Patrick Carroll had conducted a makeshift search for Russell Chandler. He had carried out the obligatory Google exploration, which revealed dozens of Russell Chandlers, including a surprising number in financial professions of one kind or another, spread from coast to coast. None that he could find had ever been involved in banking in La Plata County, Colorado.

He felt like the small dog chasing a large truck, the young reporter occasionally reflected. He would not know what to do if he caught it. He believed he could eventually figure out what to do, though. He would ask this Chandler what his role had been in the political demise of Daniel Sheridan. It was that simple.

When he asked Professor Smithson's advice, the professor laughed. Okay, let's spin this out. You find this big-time financier at some gigantic investment bank in New York and you do what?

I call up and ask for an appointment, Patrick said.

"Mr. Carroll, is that your name?" his executive assistant will ask. You say yes. The assistant says, "What may I tell Mr. Chandler is the purpose of your call?"

Patrick said, I wish to speak with him, in person if possible, about his banking experience in Durango, Colorado, some years ago.

The professor spluttered. "His banking experience… where did you say?"

In Colorado, in Durango, he owned a bank there about fifteen or more years ago.

The assistant says, "Mr. Chandler is quite busy these days. Perhaps you could just let me know what exactly you are looking for and I can tell him. Even better, may I suggest you simply send Mr. Chandler a letter with whatever questions you may have. I'm sure he'll try to find time to respond, though…let's see…he does have a rather extensive calendar of foreign travel coming up, so it might be some time." The professor said, Then you say what?

Patrick said, But it is very important that I speak to Mr. Chandler. It has to do with some serious matters that occurred in Durango when he was living here. Just before he left.

"Mr.…Carroll was it?" the assistant will say, "What exactly is your interest in this rather mysterious matter? I'm afraid I cannot help you unless you are more clear about your purpose."

Patrick said, I will be direct. I will say that I am a reporter with the *Durango Herald* and I am looking into a story having to do with Mr. Chandler's former wife and a local man—

Bang, the professor said.

Bang? Patrick looked confused.

That's the sound of the phone hitting its cradle, the professor said.

But Patrick Carroll was not easily deterred. Some days later, it suddenly occurred to him that he could seek a favor from a former roommate at Fort Lewis College who had gone to work for a national investigative firm. He googled the firm and discovered that one of its specialties was tracing lost or missing persons, having mostly to do with civil litigation. He correctly suspected that this had to do with runaway fathers and husbands. But it didn't matter. Tracing people was tracing people.

He tracked his roommate down to the Kansas City office of the firm and called him. That's five thousand, his friend Mitch said.

Five thousand what? Patrick asked.

Dollars. Just to locate this guy. Quite a bit more if you want a D&B—

A what?

Dun and Bradstreet, his friend said. Full financial work-up. That's another five. Then, if you want us to carry out a little loose surveillance—you know, see who he's with, where he eats, stuff like that—that's a good deal more. But this month's blue ribbon special, including, you know, phone calls, a few office tapes, that kind of stuff, that'll cost you real money. But let me tell you, you can pick up some really good stuff.

No, no, God no, Patrick said. It's not that kind of thing. I'm just working on a story about some bad politics here years ago, and he ought to know something about it.

So, you just want the basic track-down for five? his friend asked.

No, Mitch, Patrick said. I don't have five.

Well, your paper ought to spring for five, Mitch said. The big papers pay a lot more than that to track down some suspect.

He's not exactly a suspect, Mitch, and the *Durango Herald* is not a big paper. I'm doing this on my own and I'm asking a favor. Just work a little magic for an old friend. There's a man here who was chased out of city and state politics and I'm trying to find out who did it and why.

You're still the crusader, Mitch said. Which is it, Woodward or Bernstein?

I've about had it with crusades, Patrick said. Those were college days. I'm just trying to find out if there's any justice left in the world.

Like I said, man, you're still the crusader, Mitch said. I'll see what I can do.

27.

What's all this about? Daniel Sheridan asked. Patrick Carroll had just called him to invite him to lunch.

Patrick said, Mr. Sheridan, I've talked with a local gentleman who wants to meet with you. It's not about the old days. It's about the Animas–La Plata. So I thought maybe we'd just have lunch.

Well, I'm not much for surprises, Sheridan said. Why doesn't this "local gentleman" just call me up and we can talk on the phone?

Mr. Sheridan, Patrick said, he has an idea about how we might get this thing solved once and for all. And he'd like your thoughts on this idea.

Sheridan pondered the invitation, then said, It might also be a good idea if you brought your professor friend along. He's always interested in big ideas. Maybe this mystery man has in mind to make some history.

That's great, Mr. Sheridan, Patrick said. How about the Ore House for lunch next Thursday? I'll get a table in the back at noon.

On Thursday, Sheridan parked his pickup on East College near the restaurant and left Toby in his customary passenger seat spot with a new bone to chew. He walked toward the back of the place and was surprised to see not only Patrick Carroll and Professor Smithson but also Walter Hurley.

Sheridan nodded to Patrick and Duane Smithson and said, Mayor.

The old man stood up and put his hand out. Daniel, it's good to see you after all these years.

Sheridan said, I guess I should have asked who your "local gentleman" was, Patrick. After a slight hesitation he shook Hurley's hand.

Duane Smithson said, I told Patrick he shouldn't surprise you. You've been known to walk out of places where there were surprises. On the other hand, we were afraid you might not show up if we told you the full cast of characters.

I haven't lost every one of the social skills, Duane, Sheridan said. I may have gone rustic, but I'm not barbaric. He studied the old man and said, You're keeping pretty well, Mayor.

You mean for an old guy, don't you, Daniel? Hurley said.

Not at all, Sheridan said. It's just that I haven't seen you for a while, and none of us are getting any younger.

The four men made their way through their sandwiches as they discussed the erratic Colorado Rockies' baseball season, the local weather and summer tourist business, and the unpredictable cattle prices.

Once the plates were taken, there was a moment of uneasy silence. Patrick, Sheridan said, if this is going to be one of your attempted trips down memory lane, then I will thank you for the hamburger and be on my way.

That's not it at all, Patrick said. Getting you together with the mayor was actually Professor Smithson's idea. And, as I told you, it has to do with the mess we're all in with the Animas–La Plata. I actually approached the professor about talking to you a few days ago and he said he wasn't the best one to do it. Everybody knows he's a leader of the opposition.

Patrick's right, Smithson said. You know I'm opposed to this thing and hope it goes away. Unlike the mayor here, who's out in front of the project boosters, I think it's a nightmare. But whether it's built or not, we can't let this town go up in political flames over it. Keeping this town together is a whole lot more important than that dam. Patrick was one of the student leaders at Fort Lewis against the project. So I told him he needed someone on the other side, someone with respect in the community to join him in bringing you in as some kind of mediator.

Sheridan said, Now wait a minute, Duane. There are more reasons than you and I can count for me to stay as far away from this dispute as I can. Nothing I'm aware of in recent times changes that at all.

The mayor spoke up. Daniel, I came here today as much as anything to tell you one thing. I'm sorry. I'm sorry for what happened to you those years ago. And I'm mostly sorry for my role in it. I was wrong. That was not the first time. But I was foolishly wrong, and it caused you great damage. Now, if I could somehow take it all back, I'd do it in a heartbeat. But I can't. None of us can. So when this young man—he gestured at Patrick—came to me recently with this idea of joining up to try to solve the Animas–La Plata, I saw it as a chance to ease my conscience, I guess you'd say. Apologizing to someone you've harmed is the hardest thing any of us has to do. But now I'm doing it.

Well, Mayor, Sheridan said cautiously, that's mighty kind of you. And though no apologies are called for, I

---

certainly welcome your generous remarks. I'd be less than honest if I didn't say that your statements back then were more or less the straw that broke the camel's back where I was concerned. When you said I should throw in the towel, I knew the whole thing was over. So, I did what I had to do. Life up Florida Road hasn't been all bad since then. But from time to time it has gotten lonely.

Apologies are not all of it, Daniel, the old man said. I don't know whether you've figured it out already or not, but young Carroll here is the late Congressman Carroll's son.

Come to think of it, Sheridan said, slightly surprised, I didn't know it. He never told me. But now I think about it, I do see the resemblance. He turned to Patrick. Your father was a great man, a strong man. He helped this area become what it is. He was a true public servant.

He was indeed, the mayor said. He and I were closest of friends. So when young Patrick came along with his idea of teaming up, I had little choice but to lend a hand. We could use his father's wisdom right now to keep this community from blowing up.

That's hard to quarrel with, Mayor, Sheridan said. But I don't know how all of those old connections bring you around to my doorstep.

It's the Utes, Daniel, the mayor said. This project started out decades ago as a traditional agricultural water project. Water for the farmers and ranchers hereabouts. Congressman Carroll kept it alive year after year with appropriations to study and re-study. But there was never enough commitment in Washington to get the thing built. And as time went on, there was less support for traditional irrigation and more for municipal use and for oil and gas

development and for storing water to be sent down to Albu-
querque and Phoenix and so on.

The professor said, Mayor, you're certainly right, but
with all due respect, we know the history. We even remember when Jimmy Carter tried to cancel the thing completely. If we hadn't fought back, we'd have lost the project
completely. Man from Georgia didn't know the first thing
about western water.

Absolutely, Professor, the Mayor said. But you're right.
I don't need to ramble on with this. The point I'm trying to
make, Daniel, is that the only way this project is finally going
to be built is with the support of your friends down there, the
Southern Utes, and their brothers the Ute Mountain Utes.

From all I can tell, Sheridan said, you're right. It won't
pay its way in crop production or even in tourism and new
housing around here. The financing now only makes sense
if the tribes can use it to develop their energy and mineral
resources.

That's where we're stuck, Daniel, the mayor said. And
that's why young Carroll and the professor and I are here to
see you. We think you can help. Hell, it's more than that.
We think you're probably the key to the whole thing.

Sheridan said, Whoa. It's too early in the day for anyone here to have been drinking. But if I didn't know better,
I might suspect it.

The minute he said this, Sheridan wished he hadn't.
The mayor was known to have a midday toddy to ease him
into the evening.

Anyway, he continued, I don't have any magical influ-
ence with the Utes.

Well, Daniel, hold on there, the mayor said. We think

you might. I've made a point to keep in touch with Mr. Maynard, and Sam says the Utes are not being offered a fair share of the project water under the proposed allocation agreements. So they won't sign on under the current formulas. And until they do, the Animas–La Plata's not going anywhere. And the longer it's stuck, the angrier people around here are getting with one another.

I haven't studied these allocation proposals, Sheridan said, and I haven't talked with Sammy about them. But he's a straight shooter, and he wouldn't advise the Utes to hold out if he didn't believe they were unfair. I'm afraid Mr. Sam Maynard is the fella you ought to be dealing with. Not me.

Sam Maynard is the best lawyer in town, the mayor said, and I wish he was representing the city of Durango or La Plata County in this matter. We'd be a lot better off. But he's not. He's representing the Utes, and their interest is his interest.

But he's also a leading community figure, Sheridan said. He doesn't want this place to blow up any more than any of us.

That's true, the older man said. But he's shown his hole card and he doesn't have any more cards to play. He says he doesn't know what else to do to get this ox out of the ditch.

The table was silent. The other men waited for Sheridan to speak.

I don't know exactly what you think I can do, he said presently.

Patrick Carroll said, The mayor and I've been talking about that, and we believe—he believes—that you can talk with the Utes.

Sheridan held up his hand. I talk with Leonard Cloud and his folks quite a lot and have over the years. I'm not about to tell them how to run their business or how much water they need or anything like that.

The mayor said, No, what Patrick meant to say is that you might be able to devise a formula that would provide the water the tribes need for their projects but that would also not drain the reservoir dry.

Sheridan shook his head again. I still don't get it. I'm no expert in water project management. And, other than some kind of general idea of the Utes' rights and needs, I don't claim any expert knowledge about what's fair to them. Seems to me what you need here is one of these expert negotiators to bring everybody together and divide up the pie.

Your reluctance is understandable, the mayor said. Would it be possible, though, for you to give young Carroll here some wisdom and guidance and perhaps, as his famous father's son, let him enter the fray on the Utes' side? I'm sure the tribe remembers what his illustrious father did for them over those many years. They would welcome, I think, his advocacy of their position. Plus, he does report for the dominant newspaper in these parts.

If you mean just give him an introduction to the tribal leaders, Sheridan said, then of course. Who wouldn't do that? But I don't have any magic formula to solve the conflict and with that he'd just be seen as another do-gooder out to be a hero...and a young one at that. God knows more people have broken their pick on this claim over the years than you can shake a stick at.

He is the son of a well-known father, a real political leader, the older man said. And with your endorsement,

Chairman Cloud and the others would have to treat him seriously.

Well, if that's all you're after, Sheridan said, you could have saved yourselves the price of the lunch. I'm always happy to make introductions in the interest of a peace treaty.

After the mayor and Patrick Carroll had left, Sheridan walked down the block with the professor. Duane, what was all that about? he asked.

Hurley couldn't bring himself to ask you to bargain with the tribe, Smithson said. He was trying to find a way to use your goodwill with the Utes and leave you personally out of it.

Sheridan said, Doesn't make a lot of sense to me, but I gave up trying to figure people out a long time ago. Leonard and his people will be polite with that young man and hear him out. But he's not going to change the course of history here.

I know, Dan, I know, the professor said. But there was another agenda at work here. Hurley has been carrying you around in his conscience all these years, he wanted to get rid of the burden. He's an old man trying to settle accounts. You're probably one of the biggest ones he's got. So even for you to sit down to lunch with him is going a long way to getting that monkey off his back.

Doesn't take much sometimes, does it? Sheridan said. If that's all that he wanted, we could have had a hamburger years ago.

28.

Mr. Murphy said, I hear the mayor and Danny Sheridan finally patched it up.

Bill Van Ness said, Well, then, we must be nearing the End of Times.

Long overdue, Sam Maynard said. Everybody else is reaching for his holster around here or filling up his pickup gun rack and here these two aging warriors are have left the war path. Maybe it will spread.

The coffeepot made a second round.

What brought about all this unexpected goodwill? Mr. Murphy asked.

I had something to do with it, the professor said. Congressman Carroll's boy, Patrick, my former student, has got himself into the middle of the Animas project history. And he's trying to figure out a way to end the war. He had the idea of going to a pillar of the community, his dad's friend the mayor, and together approach Dan about bringing the Utes around.

Sam Maynard snorted. What's that about the road to hell being paved with good intentions? I'm not making any official pronouncements in this august assembly, he said, gesturing around the table, but the Utes will come "around," as you put it, when they are treated fairly. Simple as that.

Anyway, the professor said, Sheridan and the mayor smoked the peace pipe, more or less, and the old man feels a lot better about things now. Dan offered to introduce Patrick to Leonard and the tribal council.

And? Sam asked.

And, the professor said, Patrick will at least offer to help any way he can. He's not under any illusions that he has any magic. But although he hasn't told me, I think this has a lot to do with trying to appease his father's memory somehow. He hasn't followed in the congressman's political footsteps, at least for now, and I believe he's just stumbling around looking for a helpful role to play.

Ah, the good intentions of youth, Bill Van Ness said. What would we do without their inherent idealism?

We'd all go straight to hell, Mr. Murphy said. We're back to the road there being paved with good intentions.

Now, Mr. Murphy, the professor said, don't underestimate idealism. When we see it in the young, we remember how much we all believed in creating a better world in our youth.

You may remember it, Mr. Murphy said, but I don't.

They all laughed. Of course you don't, Mr. Murphy, Sam said. You missed the idealism gene altogether. You went from kid to cynical old man overnight.

Well, you have to be realistic in this life, Mr. Murphy said. You go around with your head in the clouds, dreaming wonderful dreams about a "newer world" or a "great society" and that "hopey-dopey" stuff and all you're really talking about is raising my taxes. I'm not fooled by any of that idealism stuff.

The professor said, Tom, do you really believe we're stuck where we are, that things are never going to get any better?

Why not? Mr. Murphy said. Do you see things getting any better? We've been fighting over Animas River water for a century and we'll be fighting over it a century from now.

Bill Van Ness poured more coffee all around. Yes, but there is progress. You live better than your parents did and so do I. So do all of us.

Mr. Murphy said, That's because I got off my butt and worked for it. Nobody did that for me. There're too many of these kids and lazy people just sitting around waiting for government handouts. He had started to include the Indians but checked himself.

The professor said, Now, Tom, the government is going to build the Animas dam, I'm afraid, and it brought the Interstate highway over to Glenwood Springs, and it cleaned up the uranium tailings outside of town—

And made me pay for all that stuff, Mr. Murphy interjected.

Sam said, I'd give my lesson in democracy right here, but you've all heard it. Anyway, so much for idealism. Young Carroll will fulfill his mission. He will probably fail. Not because my clients are against idealistic youth, but because they are, as Mr. Murphy says, "realistic."

29.

Daniel Sheridan asked his friend Duane Smithson to drop by the ranch for a beer.

Duane, he said, as they sat by the Florida stream, help me understand the Utes' position on the water issue.

They're in a totally new situation, the professor said. You know they've had virtually nothing all these years, and they've tried to make the best of it. They've been a lot more patient with us then we've been with them. I'd say our attitude over most of those years has been casual neglect.

But then they got the rights to all those minerals, and energy prices shot through the roof, Sheridan said. Now they're in the catbird seat. Right?

Not exactly. These are by and large thoughtful people. They've been watching us—the immigrants—all these years as much as anything to see what *not* to do as to learn what they should do. And they've seen our prosperity and our farming and our markets and our big houses and cars. And who wouldn't like to have all that? But they've also watched the price we're willing to pay for all that. Not just dollars. But the obvious costs to the air and the water and the land.

Sheridan said, Two Hawks is the best preacher I've ever heard on this.

He is, indeed, the professor said. It's pretty commonplace by now to talk about the devil's bargain we struck when we put science and technology ahead of nature beginning a couple of centuries ago. The native people didn't do that for the simple reason they never had a chance to do it. So they've been stuck, you might say, in the old ways. Nature, the mother, is where life comes from, and if you screw up nature you're screwing up life itself.

Little hard for us to reverse course now, isn't it? Sheridan said.

The irony is that the Utes are poised on the cusp of the so-called Enlightenment three centuries after the rest of us, and they're trying to figure out which way to go. The professor finished his beer, and Sheridan dug in the icy cooler for a replacement.

Leonard wants to see me, Sheridan said, and something tells me it's about their choices now. What do you think I ought to tell them? Any history lessons that might help out?

Well, Smithson said, if I were offering such advice, I'd probably say something like this. You've got two...no, maybe three choices. One is, you can develop these natural resources full steam—like we, the so-called white people, have done—and all be rich for generations to come. Settle down for the rest of your lives in the lap of luxury. Turn the res into a resort and only let your friends visit. The other option is you can sit on the resources you have and wait for time, and human greed, to bid up their price. Preserve your options and wait to decide which way to go. In the meantime you're keeping your bargain with nature. You're not rushing headlong into the commercial and material world.

Sheridan said, I suspect the tribal council has figured out those two options already. You said you thought there was a third one.

The third one, as you might expect, is a compromise between the two, the professor said. I've studied the history of these parts all my life and, as you know, I've written more books on the subject that anyone will ever read. What I've learned from all that research is a pretty basic human truth: people—maybe just Americans—don't know how to reach a balance between the old world of nature and the new world of technology. It seems to me the Utes are kind of like flash-frozen dinosaurs, if you'll pardon the expression. They are frozen examples of the prescientific world who suddenly find themselves waking up to vast undeveloped resources—riches—that offer them the chance to leap, overnight, into the world of commerce and consumption.

Right, Sheridan said, so what's the trick? Leonard would be the first person to tell you he's no smarter than the rest of us. If our tribe couldn't figure out how to use resources without destroying their source, how can we expect their tribe to do it?

Well, I'll give you one man's opinion, for whatever it's worth, the professor said. The key is that their beliefs about nature are different from ours. You know as well as I do that they think tearing up the earth, leaving scars all over the place, dumping pollution in the stream, and putting chemicals in the air is wounding a living thing, the most important living thing. If you do that, it is evil. That gives them an outlook the rest of us "enlightened" souls don't possess.

If and when they decide to pursue what I'd call the balance option, he continued, they have to use the ancient wisdom combined with the best modern techniques to protect the earth. Now, your mining experts and energy development companies are going to resist this like crazy. They'll tell the tribe all about "efficiency" and mass production methods that get the most bang for the buck—the most dollars for the least expenditure at the fastest pace. That's called modern industry. It's the culmination of enlightenment thinking transposed to the commercial world.

So, the Utes have to insist that the resources are extracted and processed with maximum protection of their land and water, Sheridan said. That will appeal to them. But something tells me they already know that. Seems like just common sense to me.

They know it, but they don't know it, Smithson said. If I advised them, I'd say let's find the best experts in the country, maybe even the world, to help us figure out if there's a better way, better than the rip-and-plunder way, to develop resources with the least possible damage. And do it in a way that shows respect for the earth, for nature.

Sheridan nodded even as he pondered this. Well, the theory of what you're talking about will appeal to them, anyway, he said. Whether it can really be done is something else.

30.

Sheridan patted the big red horse on the rump and said, Let's go. He was traveling light. He didn't take the packhorse and all the gear. He had a bedroll, his fishing tackle, some collapsible cooking gear, and a slender fish-filleting knife strapped to his ankle. He settled the Winchester in its scabbard, just in case. Toby the border collie leaped with joy when his master invited him to come along.

Both the horse and the dog could find the high lake in total darkness. But this morning was bright and sunny, a beautiful early August day.

They made their way to the lake by early afternoon and Sheridan staked the horse out on a long rope in the middle of a lush stand of tall wild grass. He tossed the bedding and cooking gear near the rock-lined fire pit he had dug out years before. He noted with satisfaction that it had not been used since his last visit. To his knowledge, Caroline was the only other person in the world who knew about this hiding place. Sheridan had discovered it in his teens and in those days had fantasized about robbing a bank in Silverton and holing up there as posses searched high and low for him.

But his interest in bank robbery disappeared quickly enough, even as his dependence on the solitude of the place increased. When he took a small tent for shelter, he rarely needed it. The moon and stars would be crystal clear. When he left the tent at the ranch, more often than not it rained or snowed, regardless of the promises of the highly skilled weather forecasters. You could pretty much depend on it.

Regardless, against great odds he took his chances and had left the tent in the barn. He took Red's saddle off and put it near the fire pit and threw his poncho—his concession to the moody weather gods—over it. He completed the ritual of firewood collection and noted happily there was more than enough nearby for his two-night stay. The many cones falling from the pines would help get things going at dinnertime. As was his custom and practice, Toby followed a yard behind his right heel everywhere he went. Toby loved the place because, even at more than nine thousand feet, you never knew when a snowshoe rabbit might hop onto the scene.

Some time before, Sheridan had put a couple of short logs across two rock piles at the edge of the lake and, as before, he picked up the fly rod and shook out a dark fly for a bright day like this. Once he had the fly tied to the leader, he sat down on the makeshift log bench and began his leisurely cast. It delighted him to see the frisky young rainbow trout break the surface across the lake as insects of one kind or another, mayflies sometimes, came within their leaping distance above the water's surface.

He was in no hurry whatsoever, but within half an hour he had three rainbow trout with a string through their gills thrashing in the shallow water. Toby, he said, say thanks to God for our dinner.

After putting the fishing equipment back in its containers, he stretched his lanky frame, working out the kinks and cramps from hours in the saddle. With Toby in attendance, he carried out his surveillance of the edges of the five or so acres of meadow surrounding the lake. As usual, he studied the soft soil at the lakeside and the edges of the tree line for tracks of creatures. It was always nice to know your neighbors, his grandfather had told him as a kid.

On the far side of the lake he paused and knelt down. Though eroded by rains, there were two distinct paw prints at the water's edge. Toby sniffed where he was looking, but the weather had also rinsed off most scents. The paws were at least four and possibly closer to five inches across. It was a sizeable cat, surely a full-grown male, and it had been there since Sheridan's and Caroline's last visit.

Sheridan studied the area more thoroughly. He could find no more paw prints. But there was a small area where the meadow grass reached the tree line where the grass had been flattened, fairly recently, by a large creature using it for a bed. He watched the grass and tree limbs and noted them swaying in a northwesterly breeze. Neither horse nor dog picked up any scent from that direction.

Toby, stay close, he told the dog. He entered the tree line where a small deer trail started and wound its way into and around the nearby craggy outcroppings. He knew the trail well and had more than once followed it as far as he could go before confronting high, steep cliff faces. He studied the narrow trail as he went, moving slowly and as quietly as he could across a surface coated with dry pine needles and pine cones that crunched loudly if stepped on.

From his earliest days, Sheridan had learned from his father and grandfather the arts and crafts of the woods. He was a better-than-average tracker and he knew the habits of the wild creatures. He had learned great respect for them, especially the predators, and it had paid off more than once. But it also paid off in avoidance of the nuisances, the porcupines and skunks and such. And after too many misadventures as a pup, Toby had learned from bitter experience to stay well away from those two creatures particularly.

Sheridan heard a snuffle from Toby and looked down to see his hackles standing up. He peered ahead and saw something in the trail, twenty yards or so ahead. It appeared to be a leather jacket covering something misshapen. He held his hand down to steady and quiet the dog and moved forward as quietly as possible.

Within ten or twelve feet he could tell it was the carcass of a young deer, probably a yearling fawn or a doe, and it had provided more than one meal for someone, almost certainly a cougar. What remained was essentially the hide and scattered bones, the larger ones of which had been worked over with very sharp teeth. The kill was recent.

Sheridan put his hand down and silently waved Toby back. He began to step back slowly himself, keeping his eyes on the carcass, when he heard a rumble. It was a unique combination of growl and deep purr, and it was coming from above him, close by. Very slowly he raised his eyes and saw the cat on a strong tree limb only fifteen or twenty feet ahead and above. It was crouched.

His first thought was Toby, but within a second he knew the dog was smart enough to take care of himself. At the same instant he instinctively reached down for the knife on his ankle and then slowly raised his arms high above his head. The Winchester was back with Red, where it was not going to do him much good in a wrestling match with this lion.

He lowered his eyes to avoid direct eye contact with the powerful creature, there to protect its kill. Before doing so, however, he saw in those familiar wide yellow eyes the natural wisdom of the ages. Though he had encountered the magnificent creatures twice before, prowling around his cattle pens in the calving season, he was startled nonetheless by the clear, mesmerizing gaze of those eyes. They would surely hypnotize you if you let them, and they took a direct gaze from a human as a challenge.

Head lowered, with eyes glancing up through thick eyebrows, Sheridan continued his retreat a step at a time, arms still raised to exaggerate his size and presence, though with little trust in that trick's effectiveness. He was simply doing what he had been taught to do under these circumstances by his predecessors and his Ute friends. He trusted also in Toby's canny trail sense not to challenge the creature.

He stepped on a pine cone, which crunched like dry cereal under his boot. He had moved to the edge of the cat's thirty-foot jumping range, and he was calculating how he would sacrifice his left arm to the cat's viselike jaws in order to get the six-inch blade under a front leg and into the ribcage near its heart. Even if successful, he would have a long ride back to town with a mangled arm and deep claw marks on his upper body, some possibly opening veins or even an artery.

Glancing up again as he retreated, Sheridan saw the cat still in its crouch. What had taken less than thirty seconds to transpire had seemed like an hour or more. He took two more quiet steps back, then saw the cat turn its great tawny head away and spring effortlessly—almost soaring—in the direction away from him and up the trail. Sheridan lifted his head and lowered his arms. Perspiration, he now felt, had soaked his shirt.

He reached down and took Toby's collar. Though the dog was making no move to follow the cat, there was always the chance that instinct might take over. Sheridan waited a full minute, then turned, and he and Toby went back down the narrow trail to the campsite.

Sheridan went to the horse and removed the Winchester. Upwind of the cat, Red had not smelled it and was calm. Sheridan pulled up its tether stake and moved it closer to where he would start his evening fire. His knowledge of the cougar told him that it would continue on its way upward into the high mountains. It had cleaned the deer carcass and had little reason to hang around to further protect its kill. And it had a range upwards of eighty square miles that it had staked out against all competitors.

Sheridan returned to the lake edge and pulled the now-quiet trout from the water, cleaned and filleted them, and rolled them in a cornmeal, flour, and salt and pepper mixture. He started the fire and watched it as it caught, blazed up, and then reduced itself to a steady heat. As he waited for the fire to abate for cooking, he retrieved his canteen from Red's saddlebag and sat on his log bench by the lake. He tipped the canteen up and felt the icy heat of the whiskey sear his throat.

Why live where he lived and why retreat to this hidden wonder if you didn't want to share it with a cougar, one of nature's most magnificent creations, he thought.

After he shared the trout, covered with fried bacon and fried potatoes and onions, with Toby, he drank half the whiskey in the canteen, then covered up for the night with his saddle for a pillow, Toby lying close to him for their mutual warmth. He never ceased to wonder at the clarity of the heavens in this place. Just before sleep, he levered a round into the chamber of the Winchester and laid it close to his other side.

31.

Guess what, Pat, my intrepid reporter? The voice on the phone that had just awakened Patrick at two in the morning sounded bright and cheerful.

The young reporter struggled to wake up and make out who this was and why they were calling.

We found him. It was his college roommate, Mitch, with the investigative firm. And you're not going to believe where he is. It's eerie, man. But he's right here in Kansas City.

Patrick tried to make sense of this. You mean Chandler? he said.

Of course, dude, isn't that who we were looking for? He's right here under our nose.

What's he doing, Mitch? I mean, what's his business? Patrick managed.

His business is making money, Mitch said in a

conspiratorial tone. What he's done all his life, apparently. He's vice president of a big investment bank and he has charge of the whole Midwest region. One of those guys who falls in a pile of poop and comes up roses. Though, apparently, his business buddies didn't ask many questions about his years down there in your place. What's it called? Durango, man, like a Western movie. Remember it well from my misspent college days.

Well, gosh, Mitch, that's great, Patrick said. You're the best.

What do we do now, buddy?

I gotta think about it, Patrick said. It's the middle of the night and it's a little hard to make a plan right now.

No rush, Patrick. This dude's not going anywhere soon. He's dug in here—chamber of commerce, charity balls, all that stuff. Big society wife too, by the way. Wasn't there something about another wife down there that I seem to remember from my little background search?

There was, Patrick said. Part of the mystery hereabouts. Let me do this, Mitch. Let's both get some sleep—this is too much like the old dorm days. Then I'll give you a call tomorrow when I've figured out the next step.

A few hours later, and after considerable caffeine, Patrick decided that he would go to Kansas City unannounced and simply walk in on Chandler. Despite the scenario Professor Smithson had projected, he felt confident he could bait the bear in his den.

A few days later, after arranging with Mitch to be sure that Russell Chandler was going to be in town, Patrick Carroll flew through Denver to Kansas City. Chandler's new wife was on the planning committee of a charity dinner the following evening, so his chances were good. Uncharacter-istically, he wore his college blazer, slacks, and tie, though they did little to improve his rumpled appearance.

He found Chandler's firm on the top floors of an ele-gant building in the Plaza shopping center, slipped past the receptionist, and confronted Chandler's assistant. I'm Con-gressman Patrick Carroll's son, from Durango, Colorado, and my father was a very good friend of Mr. Chandler's, he explained. I'm sorry I didn't call ahead, but I was unexpect-edly passing through town and wanted to pay my respects to my father's old friend.

The woman seemed perplexed but said, Just a minute, and disappeared. He could hear a discussion in the large corner office and presently Russell Chandler appeared. He wore a hesitant smile that failed to mask his perplexity. Mr. Carroll, is it? he asked as he extended his hand.

Patrick confirmed his identity and repeated his desire to meet a good friend of his late father.

I'm sorry, Mr. Carroll, Chandler said, but I hate to say that I didn't know your father—late father—all that well. When we...when I moved to Durango years ago, he was retiring from office and then soon passed away, I regret to say.

Well, he always spoke very highly of you, Mr. Chan-dler, Patrick said. He used to tell us that it was high-caliber newcomers like you and Mrs. Chandler that would make Durango a great city.

Chandler glanced back at his office and started to retreat. In any case, Patrick, he said, it was kind of you to drop by. I greatly appreciate it.

Mr. Chandler, would you mind if I just had a private word with you? Patrick quickly asked. I have a question about my father in those days that you might help me with.

Chandler reluctantly invited the young man to follow him into his office and Patrick closed the door behind him. Mr. Chandler, he said, the thing is that my father was one of the original supporters of the big water project there in our town, and when I was a young kid I know it got very heated, very controversial, and I couldn't quite get my dad to sort it out for me. And it's important because it seemed somehow to break his heart when things went bad. And I know you—and the previous Mrs. Chandler?—were there in those days and might just kind of help me understand what all happened back then.

Chandler shook his head in annoyance. I'm sorry, he said brusquely, I'm afraid it was long ago and I was only a bystander, a new banker in town, and I really didn't know much about a lot of the things that were going on behind the scenes. I do recall it got rather messy. But I never quite understood why or how. I'm sorry I can't help.

Patrick persisted. Wasn't there something about a man named Sheridan, or something like that? Wasn't he involved in some kind of scandal? I remember my father mentioning it, but I was just a kid and never could figure it all out.

Chandler's face darkened. There may have been, he said. It was long ago. He was some kind of official or other. Somebody said he took money. It was pretty awful. But I only followed it through the papers.

But didn't you actually leave about that time? Patrick asked. They were still standing. Chandler had not asked him to sit down. Part of the confusion around that time, he continued, had to do with this man Sheridan's situation and your...departure—I heard pretty abrupt departure.

That was a long time ago, Mr. Carroll, Chandler repeated. So it is of no current interest to me and, as I have said, I knew nothing about it.

Patrick knew he had only a minute or two left. But Mr. Chandler, my dad said you were right in the middle of it. That you may have sent an accusing letter about this man Sheridan. That Mrs. Chandler was somehow involved. Could all of that possibly be true? I know my father was a very honest man. He wouldn't have told my mother those things if he hadn't believed them.

Young man, Chandler said, as he moved toward the closed door, you are treading on very old and, if I may say so, very treacherous territory. Reputations can be damaged by pursing things like this.

You mean, like Mr. Sheridan's reputation?

What is your purpose here, young man? Chandler was now clearly irritated and defensive. I don't know what you are trying to achieve here, but I'm not interested in helping you do it.

Mr. Chandler, I'm just trying to find out what happened years ago in my hometown regarding a major public project my father had a great interest in. Nothing more. This project has now become even more controversial and is dividing our town. I want to find out why.

Chandler recovered some composure and said, Well, that is very laudable and I wish I could be of help. But I've told you all I know.

Patrick played his last card. Mrs. Chandler—that is, the previous Mrs. Chandler—thinks you have a great deal of information.

Chandler said, What? She thinks what? How do you know her? Have you talked to her? We're divorced, as you must know, he said heatedly. I have not seen her or talked to her since then. But she is not a woman to spread rumors or gossip. She would not do that.

She has told someone I trust, a very important person in our town, that you are the one who sent a letter to the newspaper accusing Mr. Sheridan of corruption. I've seen that letter, Mr. Chandler, and it alleges that Mr. Sheridan was taking money from investment people to pay off tribal council members and to pay blackmail to someone who would claim that Mr. Sheridan and your wife were having an affair.

Chandler now combined anger with the confusion of the trapped. I don't know what you think you're doing, Mr. Carroll, but you have no right to be here or to make these outrageous allegations, especially so many years later. My relationship to my former wife is my business and no one else's. I doubt she said what she is supposed to have said, even to one person, but if she did, she is clearly trying to settle old scores with me. I'll have none of it.

What if it could be proved that you wrote that letter, Mr. Chandler? What if it came out that you did it?

Leave now, Mr. Carroll. You are here under some kind of false pretenses. You are trying to trap me for reasons I cannot begin to fathom. Regardless of these wild statements, you have no proof of anything and you never will. Now you must leave.

Patrick started for the door. All I can say, Mr. Chandler, is that you should at least have used a typewriter. Perhaps you were too angry or too jealous to think of that. But you have very distinctive handwriting.

Who sent you here? Who's behind this scurrilous activity of yours?

No one sent me, Mr. Chandler. I came on my own. But by the way, I'm a reporter for the *Durango Herald,* and I am in fact Congressman Carroll's son. I think you might find yourself back in the spotlight down our way pretty soon. And this time you won't be able to run away.

As Patrick made a hasty retreat from Chandler's office, he heard his quarry shout something after him. Though it shocked him, it made him smile.

32.

That same night, Sheridan and Caroline had dinner at the Strater Hotel on Main Avenue. The place was a fixture. Henry Strater built it using red brick and Colorado sandstone in 1887, and it possessed—and had preserved as if in amber—all the Victorian hallmarks of that era, including the nineteenth-century furniture decorating all the rooms. Though it was a must-see on all the tourist brochures, they nevertheless had a drink in the Diamond Belle Saloon on the hotel's street-level corner. It was always worth a chuckle to see newcomers enter the Old West swinging doors from the sunshine outside and try to accustom their eyes to the earlier-century interior, part history and part Hollywood.

When the crowds began to gather, they retreated to their back corner table in the Mahogany Grill dining room. Been up to your hidden lake recently? Caroline asked.

Just last weekend, as a matter of fact, Sheridan said.

Hasn't changed much since you saw it. Probably won't change much until the next ice age.

Caroline said, I'm a paid-up member of the climate change heretics. Ice isn't going to be the problem. Your little lake could well dry up from the heat.

Hope not, Sheridan said. It'd be a real shame, now wouldn't it? It's a pretty perfect place just the way it is. I'd hate to see it turn into some kind of high country desert up there.

Then you better turn down your thermostat and go back to your kerosene lamps, she said. The projected numbers on warming don't look very good.

I do my part, Sheridan said. I keep the place pretty cold even in the winter—

Don't I know, she laughed.

And I do still have the old-timers' kerosene lanterns. Could have used one of those last weekend up above.

Why's that? she asked.

Had company up at the lake, me and Toby and Red. Big old cat up there dining out on a deer.

My God, she said. Did you see him?

Oh, yeah, he said. Saw him real good and up close. Sheridan recounted his confrontation, adding a bit to the size of the cougar and his closeness to it.

She shivered involuntarily. Maybe I won't be going back up...not that I've been invited recently. Between giant cougars and water—what do you call them—water "finortens" or some such, I may be too citified for your hideout up there.

You don't need to worry about it, Sheridan said. Between Toby and me and the Winchester, I think we can protect you from the cat. Now those finortens are a different thing altogether. But give it some thought. In another two or three weeks, it's going to begin to get cold up there at night. Even old broken-down cowboys can only put out so much warmth.

They combined their locally grown steaks with a fair red wine and celebrated with a dish of ice cream. What are you going to do about the mayor and Patrick trying to make you the peacemaker? Caroline asked.

Not much, he said. They have some fanciful notion that young Carroll can use his father's credibility to convince the Utes to accept a deal. But it seems like kind of a fool's errand to me. The young man is certainly well intentioned and carries some kind of cause left over from the congressman's day. But he's got a few years to go before he becomes a figure with the gravity required to knock heads together and settle this once and for all.

My impression—, she began.

From the omniscient Mrs. Farnsworth, I presume, he said with a smile.

Omniscient is a pretty big word for a broken-down old cowboy, she said. Anyway, she is my best source of news around here, both printed and otherwise. My impression, received from her, is that the young man and the old man are really after you. The theory seems to be, or at least Frances's theory seems to be, that by taking Patrick in hand down to see Mr. Cloud and the tribal council, you would find yourself working out an agreement, whether you intended to or not.

Sheridan said, The mayor and the boy—sorry, young man—are operating under the impression I have some clout with the Utes. It may make a nice story, but it's way

out of proportion to reality. Leonard and I are friends and
have been most of our lives. But I have no evidence he sees
me as anything other than a friend.

Daniel, she said, laying her hand on his arm. I've said
this before and I'm going to say it again, because it's the
truth. Most people around here, and certainly the Southern Utes, think you were the victim of an injustice. All
that happened back then—and believe me I carry my own
sense of guilt about it—shouldn't have happened. And it
certainly shouldn't have driven you from public life.

Wait a minute, Sheridan said. I will say this just one
more time. I'm not any kind of victim, and I wasn't driven
anywhere. I made my own choice. And it was mine alone.
When things get toxic, so ugly you can't manage it, it's time
to step away. That's all I did. No one drove my anywhere.
And whether it was just or unjust isn't for me to say. I did
what I did and that's that. I don't have any need to pick up
where I left off, or seek acceptance or approval from anyone, or reenter the public wrestling match. I'm happy the
way things are—he laid his hand on top of hers—particularly the way things have worked out now.

Still, she said. Durango is your place. It's your family's
place. You don't want to see bad feelings build up to the
point people won't speak to each other or cross the street
to avoid old friends. That's not Durango. It's not why we
live there. If I wanted to live among layers of ancient feuds,
there are lots of cities in this country to move to.

Alright, listen, Sheridan said, leaning forward. This
is between us and, at least for the time being, I'd just as
soon that Frances Farnsworth didn't know about this. I've
asked Leonard and Sam Maynard to get together down in

Ignacio in the next couple of days and see what can be worked out. I'm going to let young Carroll try to do whatever he wants to do. But after we've played out that little drama, we're going to go over several formulas for allocating the water. We're going to try to find the one that protects the Utes' interests first and is also fair to Durango and La Plata County.

He emptied the wine bottle into their glasses, and Caroline said, Daniel, I'm so happy. It is your role and your mission.

Don't get carried away with roles and missions, he chuckled. It's just a guy trying to do a job. I may pretend I don't care what's going on around here, but I do. And you know I do. Most of the time I spend up at the end of Florida Road is time spent trying to figure out just how we work ourselves out of this situation.

I know you do, she said and smiled more with her deep brown eyes than her lips. He wondered if it was the light or the wine that made her eyes shine.

33.

You did what? Mrs. Farnsworth asked incredulously.

Patrick reported on his trip to confront Russell Chandler in considerable detail, including the enlistment of his friend's search firm. I frightened him, he concluded.

It was two days after his return from Kansas City, and they sat on the Farnsworth porch in the late August afternoon. Patrick, she said, drink that beer before it gets warm and tell me exactly what happened.

He recounted the entire episode for the third time, and she shook her head. At the very least, she said when he finished, I hope you didn't claim to represent the paper. He could sue us for harassment.

He would lose, Patrick said with confidence. Even if I were wearing my reporter hat, I was within my First Amendment rights to ask him questions. He didn't have to answer. And after a few minutes he clearly wouldn't. But I basically said I was trying to sort out a complicated set of circumstances that related to my father's political history and wanted to find out what he knew. It had the benefit of being mostly true.

It is not wise to tell a falsehood, Patrick.

We can tell a falsehood, Patrick responded, when it will bring about our salvation.

Mrs. Farnsworth could not think of a response to that. They then discussed Chandler's explosion at the mention of the mystery letter.

Patrick, the elderly woman said, to my certain knowledge only two people saw the anonymous letter that accused Mr. Sheridan years ago. Myself and my late husband. How in the world could you have known it was handwritten?

I didn't, he said. I was bluffing.

34.

Alright, Leonard, Sheridan said, let's spread out these maps and see what we can invent. They were in the tribal chairman's office at Southern Ute headquarters in Ignacio, gathered around a table with tribal attorney Sam Maynard and two other tribal council members close to Cloud.

The parameters of their deliberations were defined by the Colorado Ute Indian Water Rights Settlement Agreement ratified by the state of Colorado, the Southern Ute and Ute Mountain Ute Indian tribes, and all the state and regional water conservancy districts in the area, including the Animas–La Plata Conservancy District, on June 30, 1986. After further amendment, it had been accepted and ratified by Congress two years later. Leonard Cloud and Sam Maynard had been leaders in obtaining congressional approval.

These complex arrangements had been required to guarantee the two Colorado Ute tribes a fixed amount of water from the Animas–La Plata and related Dolores River projects in exchange for the tribes' general commitment not to press their ancient tribal water rights in the courts, where the political leaders of the state and the region feared they might prevail.

A project originally designed to provide irrigation water for southwestern Colorado in the 1960s had, by the 1990s, produced a feasibility study that showed irrigated agriculture in the area would produce only about thirty-six cents in benefits for every dollar of construction and operation costs to the government. Even the most powerful Colorado senators and congresspersons could not persuade their colleagues to appropriate funds based on such economics.

Thus, what had started out as a water project for farmers and ranchers in 1968 had now become a project primarily for Indian tribes to develop their resources. Agricultural interests, originally in the forefront of boosting the project, and tourism and recreational interests who had earlier seen expansionist benefits from the water storage project, were now much less enthusiastic. Therefore, public support for the Animas–La Plata was greatly diminished, and anyway, federal dollars were now harder to come by.

All this drawn-out economic evolution caused further feasibility studies to be carried out, and in the early 1990s the Animas–La Plata, originally designed to store 192,000 acre feet of water, was now reduced to a storage capacity of 120,000 acre feet, of which some 57,100 acre feet of water would be diverted from the river system and stored annually for the municipal and industrial uses of the Southern Utes and the Ute Mountain Utes to the west.

At the same time, demand for municipal and industrial water was increasing in southwestern Colorado as elsewhere and more on the energy-rich Southern Ute reservation than even in the city of Durango. Of the 57,100 acre feet for the tribes, the Southern Utes were to receive 26,500 acre feet of water for their towns and resource development and a small amount, 3,400 acre feet annually, for a modest increase in agricultural irrigation.

The settlement also provided $60.5 million to be divided between the two tribes for commercial and community development. The Southern Utes used a portion of this amount to finance their startup development company, Red Willow.

All this was well and good, at least on paper, except for one rather crucial element: there still was no Animas–La Plata project, and the Southern Utes had been waiting a good number of years since waiving their historic water rights in anticipation of water from the project. Leonard Cloud and Sam Maynard had gone to Washington, yet again, to testify before congressional committees. The tribal chairman was succinct: "The Southern Ute Tribe will not allow the United States government to again break a treaty obligation to the Indian people." And to put a finer point on it: "We are not willing to repeat the mistakes of the past with regard to *our* water."

The presence of the possessive pronoun in the last phrase was not accidental, nor was its significance lost on members of Congress, even including those who thought Indians still wore headdresses and buckskin and rode horses.

Leonard Cloud was exasperated. What do we do, Dan? I've got tribal members who think the Great White Father in Washington—he articulated this phrase with disdain—has taken us to the cleaners yet again. We sign this agreement not to perfect our water rights in the courts in exchange for water from a project that may not be built. It looks like we've lost again. And here we've got all this coal and oil and gas and no water to develop it. It looks to us like the political "leaders" in Denver and Washington have suddenly lost interest in this water project now that it's primarily for us Indians.

Leonard, that's what we're here to try to figure out, Sheridan said. We need to think creatively, maybe even come up with a new political coalition.

He studied the proposed project maps on Cloud's table, tracing the pipeline routes that would connect the Ridges Basin Dam south of Durango with the reservation on whose northern boundary it was to be located.

I spent last weekend up in the high country letting the cougars see if I had gotten too old to eat, and I had a chance to think this over, Sheridan said. I don't know whether Sammy would agree or not, but it seems to me we have to do at least two things. We have to make our support coalition bigger. And we have to get the local folks back in the game. For example, let's propose to the Bureau of Reclamation that all these agreements be amended to bring in the Navajos down in New Mexico and some of the local water districts. Unless I'm badly mistaken, there's enough unallocated water, even with the smaller storage dam, for some small allocations, and what you've done is expand the base of people who've got an interest in seeing the project go forward.

Makes sense, Sam Maynard said. We thought about doing that a while back but couldn't get much interest among the water powers. Let's see how much we've got to divide up. He thumbed through a very thick briefing book and a stack of files in his overstuffed brief case. Finally he came up with a file of water storage figures.

Okay, as far as I can tell just eyeballing this thing right now, it looks like we might have about 25,000 acre feet a year to spread around without shortchanging either Ute tribe.

Leonard Cloud said, So, we have our brothers the Navajo, the San Juan Water Commission in New Mexico, and the Animas–La Plata Conservancy District itself to bring into our coalition.

Sheridan said, Let's divide up the 25,000 acre feet this way, just in round numbers. From what I have heard, the Navajo Nation would get on board, together with the New Mexico congressional delegation, if we ran a pipeline from here, he indicated Farmington, down to here, indicating Shiprock, New Mexico, and gave them around 5,000 acre feet a year. Sam, let me know if I'm wrong, but the San

Juan Water Commission could come back in for about 10,000 acre feet. Then the state of Colorado could use 5,000 or so acre feet for its parks and recreational use. And the Animas–La Plata Conservancy District could get about half that, which they've been trying to get. And then some spare change for that little water conservancy district down in New Mexico.

Leonard Cloud said, Sam, can we do that without sacrificing our guaranteed rights?

I hadn't thought about it before, but the answer is yes, Leonard, Sam said. I like Dan's theory. Spread the water around and develop a new constituency coalition to get financing for the project. This way, instead of going from a Durango white-guy project to a Ute project, we convert this to a white-guy-and-Ute project. It's a compromise that costs us little or nothing.

Leonard said, Why are you smiling?

Because I should have been smart enough to think of it, Sam said, and I didn't.

Leonard Cloud said, Maybe we ought to pay Mr. Daniel Sheridan the legal fees this month.

35.

The men ordered in some coffee and spent another couple of hours going over the water numbers and discussing political strategy. By late afternoon they had agreement that it was worth a try as a new approach to put the Animas–La Plata project back in play, break the stalemate, and relieve heightening tensions in the community. Leonard Cloud and his tribal council would hold talks with the Navajo Nation in New Mexico to bring them on board politically.

As he left Ignacio, Sheridan found himself a dusty block or so from Two Hawks' small house. He left the main street and pulled up in front of the old man's place. He waited for two or three minutes and then the thin arm appeared in the door and waved him in.

Two Hawks greeted him and gestured to a sagging chair. How are things at the top of the Florida these days? he asked.

Sheridan said, Me and the cows are doing fine up there. After a moment he continued, I went up to that place, that lake I told you about, in the high country a couple of days ago. Ran onto a big old cougar in a tree.

The old man's eyes wrinkled. Did he eat you?

No, but he sure could have if he decided to.

He was wondering why you would trespass on his territory, Two Hawks said.

I reckon that's so, Sheridan said. I did my best to be polite and apologize for the intrusion.

From the looks of it, it must have worked, the old man said, his eyes still smiling.

What does a creature like that think when he sees one of us? Sheridan asked as he gestured at the two of them.

No way to know, Two Hawks said. He's probably wishing you'll go away and not cause him any trouble. Shoot him or something. They've roamed these parts longer even than my own people. We've chased them up into the high country pretty much. They still survive in spite of all our efforts to get rid of them.

He still sees the natural places as his territory, doesn't he? Sheridan said.

Two Hawks said, He does. It's who he is. It's in his nature. He's free up there, just like he used to be free everywhere. He gestured in a big circle over his head.

Sheridan said, He'd pretty much cleaned up a young deer up there. But he was still hanging around. Wasn't much left to eat.

He still thought you were there to take it, Two Hawks said. We're the same way. Only it's not about food anymore. It's about our cars and TV boxes and little treasures like that. Somebody tries to take them, we kill them. After a minute or two of quiet, the old man asked, Did you leave?

I left that spot, slowly but quickly, if you know what I mean, Sheridan smiled.

That's the way to do it, Two Hawks said. You show respect by moving away. But you should never show fear. Anyway, he knows you're afraid. He can smell it.

Sheridan chuckled. I'm sure he could. My mind wasn't afraid, but the rest of me was. But I didn't leave that lake site. It's kind of gotten to be my church, I guess you'd say. It's where I go to think and...you might even say to pray, though it's not like regular church service prayer.

Two Hawks nodded. I know that kind of prayer, he said. It's my kind also. It's my peoples' kind of prayer. That is, until the missionaries gave us their kind of religion.

Well, I'd like to know, was I wrong to stay up there, in the cat's place? Sheridan asked. I ate my supper and curled up by the fire for the night. He could have jumped me in the night pretty easily.

Two Hawks' eyes wrinkled again. He watched you.

He watched you all night. You weren't afraid anymore and he could tell that. I suppose he was thinking if you didn't want to harm him, why should he harm you? Besides—the holy man smiled—he already had his supper.

Sheridan said, It was very strange to share that place with the lion. It was his place. It still is his place. But that place has been a comfort to me in some bad times. And a pleasure in better times.

So long as you don't spread poison around or shoot the place up, he'll share it with you. Just treat the water and the trees and the grass with respect. I know you well enough to know you will clean the place up when you leave and restore it to health. That's all that cat creature cares about. He's the king there. It's his kingdom. You must respect it. If you do, he will respect you.

The two men sat in silence for a while. Then Two Hawks said, You're trying to help us with the water, I guess.

Sheridan had no notion of how the old man could have known that. I just gave Mr. Cloud and his people some ideas, he replied. That's what I was doing up in the high country. Thinking about this. There's some water to negotiate with and I thought it might be spread around a little for everyone's benefit.

Two Hawks nodded. I suppose that makes sense. Benefit as many as possible. But when these engineers start moving their big machines around, just remember to respect the water. It is sacred, especially in these parts. We will all be judged, including my people, on whether we treat this water, this gift, with respect. Maybe even a kind of reverence. Without this water there is no life.

Over his many years with Two Hawks, Sheridan

anticipated the moment and stayed silent. The old man bowed his head, then looked up. He raised both hands and began a slow, quiet chant. It was mostly in the native language. But from time to time Sheridan could make out English words...*pray,* and *the land,* and *earth and sky,* and *all the creatures.* He always seemed to want to hold his breath when this happened, not to break the spell.

After a moment's silence, Two Hawks moved his raised palms in Sheridan's direction. He asked for a blessing on his friend. He thanked the Spirit for sending this man to help his people. He said that Sheridan was worthy of a blessing, that he respected the natural world and all the creatures in it. He asked the Spirit to go with his friend Sheridan and always be with him.

The prayer ended and Sheridan breathed out. They then got up, and Sheridan went to the open door. Two Hawks said, Take care of yourself. And give that cougar lots of room.

36.

My turn to cook, Sheridan said to Caroline on the phone. Jameson at six and elk sometime after that. See you Friday. And, by the way, bring your new painting to show me. I haven't seen any in a while.

A few minutes after six that Friday, she drove off Florida Road through the Sheridan ranch gate. Toby bounded up, happy to see his good friend. She had a brown-paper bundle under her arm.

She put the bundle on the dining room table, knowing from history that they would eat in the kitchen, and he embraced her. It lasted a long time. Uncharacteristically he said, I guess I've missed you.

She laughed. You guess? Either you did or you didn't. Oh, well. Always the cowboy. Never comfortable with affection.

I'm comfortable with affection, he said, patting her backside. I'm just not always comfortable talking about it.

You manage your demonstrations of what you call affection, she said, in a way that gives you a chance to see if I've gained weight.

Now Sheridan laughed. Not my purpose. I hope to have a chance to make a more thorough inspection later. But in the meantime, you haven't. Just so you understand, I pat Red on the rump too, and it's not to see whether he's gained weight.

You cowboys, she laughed. All alike. About as romantic as a slipped disk.

He turned, took her wrist and pulled her into his arms, and kissed her for a considerable length of time.

Well, she said, that's a little more like it. Now I know you are glad to see me.

He poured the whiskey neat into two water glasses and added a couple of cubes of ice to hers. They touched glasses and drank.

She gave him a report on her painting excursions and announced that this was a celebration. The fine arts gallery in town had bought a half dozen of her paintings and were going to exhibit them the coming weekend. He toasted her success and congratulated her. She brought in the bundle and untied it. She had another four paintings, like the others, roughly two feet by a foot and a half in dimension.

They're beautiful, he said studying them one by one, just like always. This one, he held up a study of a doe and twin fawns against an aspen grove, it's spectacular. Look at those trees. The sunlight on those leaves is just real. And those deer are going to jump off that canvas. How do you do that? It's amazing. You're just getting better and better. No wonder those art folks scoop these up. You're going to be a famous artist. Fancy dealers from the city are going to be after you.

She shook her head, but he continued with a long face. Then, I know what'll happen. You'll be hobnobbing with those arty people in New York and San Francisco and all your small-town cowboy friends will be forgotten. He pulled a large red handkerchief from the back pocket of his worn jeans and put it to his eye.

She laughed out loud. Oh, now look at him. Weeping in his beer at his lost love. She took his face in her hands and now gave him a long, soft kiss. Poor cowboy, she said. Poor, sad cowboy. Taking all this drama in, Toby stood up in the doorway and barked.

They both laughed and sipped their whiskey. I mean it about these pictures, he said. Lord knows I don't understand art. But as the fella said, I know what I like.

Take your pick, she said.

Oh, I couldn't do that, missy, he said. These are much too valuable to be tossing around like that. Though I would like to put this one with the deer and aspen trees up on that wall in there, gesturing toward the dining room, where folks could see it.

Folks? she laughed. What folks? If you have folks in here, it's sure not when I'm around. She turned her mouth down. Unless...

Unless what? he said.

Unless, you know, some other cowgirl's taking my place.

Now, missy, you're risking a swat on the behind for talking like that.

What is it with my behind, mister? she said. You seem to have it on your mind.

Because I haven't seen it in too long, he said. He refilled the glasses and turned on the low fire under the elk steaks.

He told her about his recent meeting with Leonard Cloud, Sam Maynard, and the council members and the scheme they had come up with to reorganize a coalition to get the Animas–La Plata finally constructed.

She clapped her hands. I knew it. I knew it. I knew if you got into this that you'd figure it out. I knew it. She then asked a number of questions, including about the federal money for construction, repayment contracts for all the users, whether current feasibility studies could be used to avoid more delays, and a variety of other issues that revealed her considerable knowledge about the project. He emphasized that it was not a done deal, that concurrence would have to be established with the other users and political approval achieved in Denver and in Washington.

During this discussion he finished cooking dinner and served it at the kitchen table. He opened the sensible red wine she had brought, noting with pleasure that there were two bottles.

They were into the second bottle, and dishes of ice cream, when she asked, Did you see Two Hawks when you were down there…in case it's any of my business?

He nodded, slightly uncomfortable at the inquiry. For him, the visits with the ancient holy man were about as close to confession, therapy, and meditation as he would ever get. It was a measure of his trust in her that he even let her know of his friendship with the old man.

I did, he said. As I've told you before, it always makes me feel better…cleaner, somehow. It's a strange thing, but I gave up trying to figure it out a long time ago. He talked to me about the cougar up above—he gestured to the north-east and the Weminuche—and how the cat was thinking. He paused, then said, I don't think any of us, white folks, non-Indians, whatever, will ever come close to the under-standing of nature and the wild creature that the Indians have. It's just so natural, I guess you'd have to say, for them. It's their culture and their history and even their blood that gives them the wisdom they have about these things, things we either take for granted or try to use or kill.

She held his hand as he talked. I'll tell you something I've never told anyone else, he continued. After I've seen the holy man, I think a lot about what he says and about his prayers and it gets to me—he pointed to his heart—here. I came back that day and Toby and I walked up the trail to the cattle grazing meadow and I sat down there and I…I…I guess I cried.

By now Caroline had tears in her eyes. She stood up, took his hand, and led him upstairs.

37.

She awoke before dawn that Saturday morning, before Sheridan for a change. She slipped from bed and smiled as he snored, then wrapped herself in his old robe.

Downstairs, she let Toby out and put coffee on. She poured orange juice and lit the fire under a large skillet. She had put strips of bacon in the skillet and stirred up the eggs when he appeared on the stairs.

Well, now, isn't this something, he said. If it hadn't been for the bacon smell I'd probably still be asleep. Did you slip something in my whiskey last night?

The elixir of love, she said. Works every time.

I'd have to say it works just about every time where you're concerned, he said as he kissed the back of her neck.

Where I'm concerned? she murmured. And what about those other cowgirls we were talking about last night? Works with them too? He started to smack her behind and she winced, There you go again. The old rump fixation.

The sun was now emerging over the ridge line that divided the Sheridan land from the Waldron place. They finished the bacon and eggs and toast, and she poured a second cup of coffee.

I had a glass of wine with Frances Farnsworth a couple of evenings ago, she said. She had some interesting information. Her enterprising reporter, young mister Carroll, tracked down my former husband.

Sheridan's jaw dropped, and he put his coffee cup down heavily. He did what? Why in hell would he go and do a thing like that?

Well, he did. He's obsessed with that business years

ago, as you know. And he apparently had the notion he could unwrap the mystery and straighten things out by talking to what's-his-name.

Russell is his name, as I recall, Sheridan said evenly.

I do recall that was his name. I guess it still is. Nevertheless, the young sleuth found him in Kansas City of all places and confronted him.

That would have been worth the price of admission, Sheridan said.

I suppose, Caroline said. In any case, Patrick Carroll trapped Russell into admitting—finally—that he wrote the letter.

With all due respect, Sheridan said, if you don't mind my saying so, my recollection of Russell was that he was not the sharpest tool in the box. But how in the world did the kid trap him, as you put it?

According to what he told Frances, Patrick told him he knew the letter was handwritten and he'd verified that it was Russell's handwriting.

No one except the Farnsworths ever saw the letter, according to what I heard, Sheridan said. It was marked personal and Murray opened it, and they printed parts of it but never showed it to anyone else. How in God's name would the kid have known it was handwritten?

He didn't, Caroline said. He was bluffing. Poor Russell bit and said he knew it wasn't handwritten, that he wasn't that dumb. Then he threw Patrick out.

Sheridan shook his head. Now what? What is Frances going to do now? If she brings all that old garbage up again, you might want to consider joining that art colony out in San Francisco.

What about you? Caroline asked.

Me? I'll pack up what I need in the panniers and Red and Toby and me will head for the Weminuche and stay for a good long while.

Daniel, wait a minute, she said. The fact that a jealous husband wrote an anonymous, libelous letter years ago will prove to the few remaining doubters in this town that you were wronged. It will set things right.

Caroline, you don't understand, he said. I don't have to prove anything to anyone, especially not this many years later. I don't care what people think. I found out a long time ago that people will believe what they want to regardless. So, the price required—digging up all the old garbage—is too high for the reward, some kind of reinstatement that I don't need and don't care about.

She touched his unshaven face. Well, my dear cowboy, it may not be your decision, or our decision, to make. Young Carroll is hardly the soul of discretion, and our friend Frances is still in the newspaper business, at least the last time I checked.

38.

Leonard Cloud and a delegation of the Southern Ute tribal council welcomed Patrick Carroll and former mayor Walter Hurley and thanked Daniel Sheridan for bringing them to the monthly council meeting. A number of tribal members were in attendance to see if any new tribal business would affect their livelihood. As usual, the setting was informal.

Sheridan explained that the mayor, at Mr. Carroll's urging, had offered their services to the Utes and the Durango community to try to resolve differences that were becoming sharper over the Animas–La Plata water project. He said that he knew the tribal elders remembered with fondness when Mr. Hurley had been mayor those years ago and how, like his friend Congressman Patrick Carroll Sr., this young man's father, he had always supported efforts to develop water for the region.

Sheridan did not say, nor did the tribe's memory require it, that during those Hurley-Carroll years, the proposed dam and water project had been primarily for businesses and farms in the Durango area north of the tribe's reservation.

Patrick Carroll thanked the tribal leadership for the opportunity to express his interest in being of service in any way that would benefit them. He pointed out his position at the *Durango Herald* and how the newspaper over the years had both championed the water project, properly designed, and urged that the two Ute tribes should receive a fair share of the stored water in the reservoir to be built.

Sheridan had explained to Leonard beforehand the clumsy behind-the-scenes maneuvering that had brought both the mayor and young Carroll to his doorstep. And this scene at the council meeting, therefore, was political theater on a small scale. After many decades, the Indians had become accustomed to accommodating the machinations of the white man's politics. Sheridan had explained that the older man and the younger man had conspired to get him involved as a peacemaker, that he had demurred and urged them both, given their histories, to undertake the mission themselves, and that he had on his own already decided to try for a political solution to the dilemma that he had in fact discussed with Leonard and Sam a few days before.

Leonard Cloud managed his role with considerable aplomb, applauding both Carroll and Hurley for their concern and their support. He reiterated the tribe's position as one of accommodation and conciliation. He urged the two men and their friend Mr. Sheridan to do all they could in the Durango community to reawaken public support for construction of the Animas–La Plata facilities, despite the fact that it had metamorphosed into what was basically now a project designed to provide municipal and industrial water for the two Ute tribes.

The former mayor responded for them both, in rotund oratory of a century before, promising utmost effort to heal the ancient wounds caused by contentious debate over the project over all these years and pointing out to one and all that a developing Southern Ute Tribe, particularly one developing needed energy supplies, was not only in the interest of Durango, but also in the interest of Colorado and the entire United States.

Patrick Carroll concluded with his commitment to do his best to see that the *Herald* continued to provide public encouragement for water for the region and for tribal projects.

Sheridan stayed behind to thank Leonard Cloud for managing the play so effectively. Leonard said, It is my pleasure. Part of modern-day politics. Thanks for bringing them around. Believe it or not, they can help out with the public relations with the old and with the young. It is funny, though, he continued, they thought they brought you here and you thought you brought them here. So now you are all happy.

Sheridan thanked him again and said, Of course they don't know I've been trying to work behind the scenes all along and as far as I'm concerned, we'll leave it at that. The tribal chairman nodded in agreement.

39.

Sheridan and Red, with Toby's help, were working his small cattle herd down from their high summer grazing area on the north end of the Sheridan ranch property, which bordered the southern end of the San Juan National Forest and on which the Sheridan family had had grazing rights for several decades.

Sheridan had found it hard to get the cougar out of his mind. The previous night, and several nights before that, he had seen those wide yellow eyes, clear, unblinking, knowing, in his dreams. They were a profound mystery. How could a creature of nature, though a proud and noble one at that, possess a look so much more powerful than any human he knew?

As he worked Red behind the herd, he wondered what the cat had been thinking and reflected on Two Hawks' remarks. He had been in the creature's territory. Quite possibly it had considered the area of the hidden lake part of its hunting range for some time. And quite possibly it had observed him on more than one occasion, including when he had taken Caroline with him, on his trips to the lake.

Though no philosopher, Sheridan had considered man's role in nature more than once. In his youth it had occupied him little. But as the years went on and he considered instruction he had received from grandfather and father alike concerning respect for the land and nature's creatures, he grew more and more—and without much reflection—to a familiarity and acquaintance with his surroundings that seemed, for lack of a better word, natural. Increasingly with age, he wanted to fit in to his surroundings, not to be separate and apart from them.

A year or two before, he had instructed Sam Maynard to draw up a will leaving his place to Caroline and asking that his ashes be scattered along the edge of his hidden lake in the Weminuche. She would know where that was and how to get there.

He now supposed that was why he was preoccupied by the cougar. He wondered, if it had come down to it, whether he would have put his blade into the great creature's heart and, if he had, would it have seemed unworthy of him to have killed such a wonder of nature for simply protecting its own territory. For Sheridan, that confrontation had become what a literary person like Caroline would have called a metaphor. If the cougar represented nature and was playing its role in that context, what were his rights and what were his responsibilities?

Sheridan slapped a recalcitrant heifer with his lariat rope, and it jumped and bellowed. The cat had rights. It had a right to be itself and to play out its purpose. Sheridan recalled a church service his father had taken him to as a boy and the sermon about man having dominion over the earth and all the creatures on it. It didn't sound right then and it sounded even less right as time went on. Man may have a right to grow crops and herd cows and make a living.

But he didn't have the right to kill one of nature's works of art, such as a cougar, out of thrill or sport or territory.

The herd made its way slowly down the slopes, stopping from time to time to pull up some particularly tasty grass, with Toby crouched to nip a heel here or there at Sheridan's command. He was in no hurry. Early fall and this minor version of the old cattle drives were his favorite times. Now, in early September, he could tell by sniffing the air that the first snow would not be long off. And the first one, for some reason, was often a big one. So the sun felt good, the cattle were healthy, and he was with his horse and dog.

He thought of Caroline. Try as he might, he had not been able to keep her at arm's distance. He smiled to himself at how shrewd she was in managing him and at how her company pleased him so much. He went out of his way to keep his emotions in check around her. But he knew she had, in that mystery of the ages, got herself into his heart. He hadn't expected it, but he knew now he would be somewhere between lonely and lost without her. He marveled at her cleverness with finance, yet her sensitivity with her portrayal of nature.

Which brought him back to the cougar. He somehow wanted to reach a basic truth about himself and the cougar, himself representing mankind and the cougar representing nature. He wasn't smart enough, he concluded, to achieve what many of the great philosophers throughout history had failed to achieve. The easy solutions were that old preacher's notion years before about man's dominion over the earth, or the other notion of not chopping down a tree or eating a steak.

The Sheridan heritage had always been to clean up after yourself and not hurt anyone downstream. They had kept their herds in check, kept animal waste and herbicides out of the Florida River, and refused to sell off their timber to the logging companies that continued to beseech them with dollars. It was nothing they prided themselves in. It was just their way and their practice.

The herd was now approaching the low pasture lands where it would winter. Some would go to market and provide enough in the bank to make it until next spring. Sheridan wondered if Caroline would like to go someplace warm, maybe down to Mexico, for a week or two when it got coldest. He hadn't done anything like that for quite a while, and she would probably never bring it up herself. But it might be nice for a change. She's probably tired of that Jameson and ready for some tequila, he thought.

Sheridan closed the gate to the high country trail, patted Toby and praised him, then gave him a fresh bone for his reward. Red got an extra helping of oats for his good work.

Sheridan shook his head. He still didn't know what to think about the cougar. It would continue to be a mystery and a haunter of dreams. Maybe that's why he was put here, he thought. Maybe his real purpose is to tell us with those luminous big yellow eyes to be careful, not of him, the creature, but to be careful how we live, what we chop down, what we eat, what we destroy so needlessly.

40.

I've finished my piece, Mrs. Farnsworth, Patrick said. It's just under five thousand words.

My God, she exclaimed. What in the world do you think you're going to do with something like that?

I was hoping you might take a look at it and consider running it as a series, the young reporter said.

She laughed. A series? Patrick, the *Durango Herald* is not *The New York Times*. We don't do "series." Besides, I've told you more than once I'm not going to print a history no one wants to read, least of all Daniel Sheridan's. It would be cruel and unnecessary. People around here—she circled her hand above her head—including particularly your generation, would think I had gone completely insane. And my late dear Murray would absolutely turn over in his grave.

Patrick rubbed his eyes, red from writing late into the night for the past two weeks and from reading and rereading old stories and new notes, and he frowned. Well, somebody has to print this, he said. Mr. Sheridan and everyone else are just the actors. This is a story about injustice, an injustice in a community as great as Durango. The point is, if it can happen in a place like this, it can happen anywhere.

Sit down, Patrick, the journalistic matriarch ordered. You have driven me into a role of delivering life lessons and it is not a role I relish. But here goes again. There is injustice in the world. It is everywhere, including in Durango. You are right. If it can happen here, it can—and does—happen everywhere. It is called life. Life is unjust. It is unfair. Our profession, my profession, claims to comfort the afflicted and afflict the comfortable. That's hogwash. We print the news. The good and the bad and, I regret to say, sometimes the untrue. Have you noticed how our little section called "Corrections" has grown? It's because we don't always get it right. In fact, she admitted ruefully, we seem to be getting it wrong more and more often.

But, Patrick interrupted, you—we—have a duty to correct things. That's what my story is about.

A one-sentence correction to yesterday's story is one thing, Mrs. Farnsworth said. Your epic history of a bygone era is quite another. Why would you want to do this? I've told you this paper does not want it and will not print it. Take a trip. Go fishing or something. Get this obsession out of your system. I have grown very fond of Caroline Chandler. I don't want her to pack up her easel and move away. I don't want to cause the Utes more trouble than they've already had to face for over a century. And I can absolutely guarantee you that you will drive Daniel Sheridan into the wilderness permanently. For what? Justice?

Truth, ma'am, truth, Patrick said quietly. The truth will set you free, or something like that. Let me tell you why I'm "obsessed," to use your word. My parents and my church and my college told me that a lie unanswered is a lie accepted. And when a person—or a town—accepts a lie and decides to live with it, it corrodes their soul. If you live with one lie, you can live with two, or a dozen. It's true of a country too. When we are told we have to make war against North Vietnam because one of their little boats fired on one of our big ones, 58,000 Americans and millions of Vietnamese died. And it was a lie. When we invade Iraq because it has weapons of mass destruction, and there aren't any, 40,000 American casualties and a trillion dollars later it is a lie. I don't want my country to live with those kinds of lies. And I don't want Durango to live with those kinds of lies either.

Mrs. Farnsworth turned away and looked from her corner office at the *Herald* toward the distant San Juan Mountains. She refused to let the young man see the tears burning her eyes. The room was quiet, then she coughed and regained her composure.

She turned back. Alright, Patrick. What's the lie? Did Russell Chandler write the accusatory letter, as we assume? Did Daniel Sheridan pay off tribal members to raise money to keep Russell quiet, as we do not assume? Did Mr. Sheridan and Mrs. Chandler have an affair? Which is really none of our business. Is it all of these? Have you proved to our readers' satisfaction, and their probable disinterest, that all of this happened or didn't happen?

No, ma'am, but what I can prove is that Russell Chandler was the frontman for an investment syndicate that was trying to corrupt the Southern Utes and steal their mineral resources and control the water from the Animas–La Plata project.

Patrick, Mrs. Farnsworth said, you better let me read what you have.

PART THREE

41.

Professor Duane Smithson and former mayor Walter Hurley had coffee cake at the local bakery for the purpose of letting the mayor recount his recent visit to the Southern Ute tribal council meeting.

I've studied the history of this region I suspect about as much as anyone around, the professor said, and you cannot understand southwestern Colorado, or La Plata County, or the city of Durango, without understanding water. Since they brought the railroad in here in 1878 and this town grew up around it, it has been all about water. If someone came in here and tried to study this community, they'd have to know water history and water law. You and I both know that more than one of the old-timers—farmer, cattleman, or miner—drew down on one another over a diversion ditch or a makeshift dam or even watering a herd of cattle.

When the great dam-building era of the twentieth century began those decades ago, he continued, it was virtually inevitable that sometime, sooner or later, there would be plans for a dam on the Animas to make the desert bloom or some such political rhetoric. What none of us expected, even say as recently as fifteen years ago, is that the project would be completed only if it satisfied the Utes' historic water rights and that they, not the wealthy folks in Durango and around, would be the principal beneficiaries.

Well, it sure as hell comes as a surprise to me, the mayor said over his breakfast. When I was mayor it wouldn't have crossed our minds. You couldn't have sold this thing to the city or the county or the state or the federals as an Indian project. Just wouldn't have happened. But here we are. And now they're in the catbird seat and can make it happen or not.

Tell me what happened when you went down to Ignacio, the professor asked.

Young Carroll and I offered our services to the Indians, the mayor reported proudly, and they seemed very pleased to have the son of a former congressman, known as one of the leaders of the "green" opposition to the Animas–La Plata, and yours truly, a stalwart over the years in support of developing our region's water rights, there before them, representing a new coalition of support.

Was there much discussion, the professor asked, about the fact that what was meant to be a dam and reservoir for Durango business and farms is now primarily a project for the Utes' use?

Not at all, the mayor said. It never came up. I guess to the outsider it would seem somewhat ironic that the Indians, who were pretty much ignored when this thing emerged on the drawing boards in '68, are now the big winners.

There is justice, after all, the professor said.

Well, you could say that, I guess, the mayor countered. But I'm one of those unreconstructed pioneers and manifest destiny believers. God put the US of A here for us to occupy and enjoy. And by God, I've enjoyed this little corner of it as much as anyone alive.

The professor said, Good for you. But I hope the time has come for the Utes to enjoy a little more of it also. And, by the way, generate some electricity with their coal and some gasoline from their oil in the process. That seems to be the American way too, last time I checked.

Yes, yes, the mayor said. What can you do when the Indians lucked out with all those energy resources? Should shut up those who've claimed all these years that we shuffled those poor nomads off into the armpits of America. They'll all be driving Cadillac cars before you know it.

The professor moved a bite of coffee cake around and thought about this. Who's to know? he finally said And it's hardly our place to tell them what kind of cars they can drive. By the way, have you ever met a Ute holy man called Two Hawks?

Can't say that I have, the mayor said. I thought I knew them all, at least the ones that came to the council meetings. But he's a new one to me.

Very good friend of Dan Sheridan's and his father before him, the professor said. If the Utes listen to him, they may hold off on the Cadillacs. He's still one of those old-timers who thinks we're supposed to be part of nature.

Yes, yes, the mayor said. Maybe so. But people are people and, when it comes to fine living, I doubt the Indians are much different from the rest of us. He paused, then said, By the way, speaking of Daniel Sheridan, he was down there in Ignacio with us. The whole purpose of this little play you helped us direct. Remember, young Carroll and I were there mostly as a sideshow to encourage Daniel to jump in and help the Indians accept the water deal the folks in Denver and Washington were offering them.

Did he jump in? Smithson asked.

Well, not exactly, the mayor said. He sat in the front

row, but over toward the side, as young Carroll and I said our piece. And he made no speeches. It was pretty clear, though, that he was paying close attention. If our little scheme works, he'll be hooked and he'll find his way back to Leonard Cloud and his folks and convince them to sign up.

The professor slurped coffee to conceal his amusement. It is certainly to be hoped, he said. It is well known that the Utes hold him in high regard. I have no doubt that they will pay very close attention to what he has to say to them, if he chooses to say anything.

The day before, the professor had encountered Sam Maynard on Main Avenue and learned that there had been a quiet, closed-door strategy session involving Sheridan at the tribal headquarters. Maynard had told him that Sheridan may have come up with a water allocation formula acceptable to the tribes that would cause them to approve the propose project if the state and federal water authorities accepted the distribution proposal. Smithson had been sworn to secrecy. And the last person he would share this very significant intelligence with was the former mayor, who broadcast more widely than the Durango radio station.

It was certainly clever of you and Patrick Carroll to come up with the scheme to bring Dan Sheridan into the negotiations, the professor said.

No, the mayor said, you get the credit, Professor. You and Patrick came to me. I was just playing the role that was written for me.

You played it superbly, Mayor, as always, Smithson said. Let's hope our reclusive friend Mr. Sheridan will play his as well. But I must tell you, he said as they left, if he does, I doubt that we will ever know about it.

42.

Norton Biggs, the chairman of the La Plata County Commission, rapped his gavel and said, Let's come to order. This commission's now in session, and Mr. Maynard, the floor is yours for your report.

Sam Maynard walked to the slender podium facing the horseshoe-shaped commissioners' table and began. I may have some good news, Commissioners, and no one is happier for it than I am.

He then gave a ten-minute history of the Animas–La Plata water project from its inception in 1968 to the current date. He used a slide projector and screens visible to the commission and to the large audience. Word had circulated that this was not going to be a normal commission meeting, and there was very little standing room at the back and sides of the chamber.

That brings us to today, Maynard said, and the dilemma we face. As you all know, the project as currently designed is principally intended to provide municipal and industrial water to satisfy the historic rights—it was noted by a few lawyers in attendance that he did not say "claims"—of the Ute Mountain Ute and Southern Ute Tribes. And both tribes have agreed to forgo any judicial process to perfect those rights, but only on the condition that the project be built and they receive the water they've been promised.

He continued, But the project has not been built, and we're in kind of a political cul-de-sac where the federal government has not guaranteed the money necessary to build the project and the Ute tribes have indicated that they may

abrogate their agreements unless it does. I don't need to tell
this commission that the longer this stalemate continues, the
more friction grows between pro- and anti-project sides in
the Durango area and between the majority community and
the tribes. There is too much resentment in this town and this
area and—he looked around—I suspect also in this room.
There were murmurs and restlessness around the room.

Alright, he said, we're here to discuss a way out, and
that's my purpose this evening. In recent days there have
been lengthy discussions with the Ute tribes at Ignacio and
Mancos. Community leaders from here in Durango and
on the reservations and yours truly have considered a wide
variety of solutions, some old, some new. And here's the
best idea we've come up with.

Maynard pressed a control and a slide appeared showing the water apportioned to the two tribes under previous
agreements but also the distribution of additional reserved
water supplies to the Navajo Nation downstream in New
Mexico and the several state and local water conservancy
districts. As he read off the numbers, people in the crowd
leaned forward and made comment to their neighbors, and
the *Durango Herald* reporter wrote furiously.

This is not rocket science, Maynard said. But it is a
demonstration of goodwill by the principal users, the Ute
tribes, and a pretty innovative, if I may say so, effort to
bring other beneficiaries into the bargain. If we can get
agreement from all concerned that they will support this
formula—and both Ute tribes have already agreed—then
we can take this proposal to state officials in Denver, to
our congressional delegation, and to the Department of the
Interior and Bureau of Reclamation.

DURANGO

The chairman interrupted him. Mr. Maynard, if what you say can be made to happen, it is certainly very good news for all of us. But doesn't the final word rest with the powers that be in Washington? They've got the purse strings.

Mr. Chairman, Maynard said, that is indeed true. But part of the reason our congressmen and senators have not been able to pass the appropriations is that their colleagues know, or have been told, that the Indians are not on board and that there is only mediocre support in this area. The approach I've outlined here this evening—and it is only an outline, with lots of footnotes and nuances not included— promises to bring full-fledged support from the tribes in addition to bringing Indian and non-Indian support from New Mexico, which we haven't had.

So, the chairman said, you're saying this county and the city of Durango and the state of Colorado and the water conservancy districts we represent all have to step up now and commit to this project along the lines you've suggested here this evening?

That's pretty much it, Mr. Chairman, Sam Maynard said. And it begins right here. There is every reason to believe that if the La Plata County Commission—you folks at this table—pass a resolution of support, certainly the San Juan Conservancy District, then the Durango City Council, and then the governor of Colorado will sign up as well.

Maynard smiled and said, Just between you and me... and these three or four hundred people behind me—there was laughter from the crowd—I've talked with everyone of those folks and they've all said if this county commission approves, they will approve.

The commissioners looked at each other up and down the table. Then the chairman said, Mr. Maynard, thank you for your time and considerable effort on this project over many years, and thank you for your presentation. We will now hear from anyone in this audience—within reason—who wishes to be heard, and we will take it under advisement.

Maynard started to turn away, then stepped back and said, Chairman, with all due respect, I cannot guarantee this coalition we've hammered together will stay hammered for long. I urge your speediest consideration—even a vote on the resolution I've presented this very evening if at all possible.

A dozen or more people queued up at the microphone, and Sam Maynard excused himself, shaking hands and receiving pats on the back as he left.

The record of the evening's proceedings did not show any reference to Daniel Sheridan. And no one was more pleased by that than Sheridan himself. Sam Maynard had told him after the Friday coffee roundtable that morning that he would propose a resolution to the county commission that evening and had invited him to come, knowing full well that the invitation would not be accepted.

Instead, Sheridan had dinner at Caroline's modest ranch house northwest of town. After he told her about Sam Maynard's scheduled appearance before the county commission, she set down her cocktail glass and said, To hell with these pork chops. Let's go down there.

He shook his head. Not on your life. Sammy will put on a show and work his magic, and if God is in His Heaven and all is right with the world, the commission may endorse this idea and we'll be on our way.

Don't you want to be there? she asked. It's historic, and you did it. You've got to be there. Despite her enthusiasm, she did not expect a positive response.

Now, missy, he said, touching glasses with her. Let's toast Sam's success and the Utes' success and leave it at that. In case you haven't noticed, I haven't been much for crowds in quite a while, and I don't see this crowd as being much different. Frankly, given a choice between a county commission crowd, particularly tonight, and that cougar up there—he gestured toward the Weminuche to the northeast—I'd take the cougar any day and twice on Sunday.

She got up to get the pork chops, kissed his cheek, and said, My dear Mr. Sheridan, you are a nineteenth-century caution.

43.

Just when you think you've seen it all, Frances Farnsworth thought to herself, something like this comes along.

Two days earlier she had received a call from Russell Chandler requesting—then demanding—a meeting with her. She wished to know the purpose and he said, You know very well the purpose. You sent that young punk reporter of yours to waylay me in my office and to accuse me of just outright unbelievable things. And I suppose you intend to print his lies without even talking to me.

She was silent on the phone for a moment, then said evenly, Mr. Chandler, what I intend to do is of interest to you only if I do it. If there is something you think I should know, I am perfectly happy to have it. But you might save yourself a trip by just sending me a letter or telling me what you wish to tell me right now.

You're damn right there are things you need to know, Chandler blustered. And I intend to say them to you directly.

Fine, I'll be in my office this Friday at noon, Mrs. Farnsworth said, then hung up.

He's here, her assistant said midday that Friday. Frances asked that he be shown in.

She did not offer her hand, nor did he. What's on your mind? she asked.

What's on my mind? he said, his face deep red. He clearly had been gathering steam for some time. What's on my mind is the scurrilous accusation of this punk you sent to see me.

Mr. Chandler, she said. I didn't send him. He went on his own. I didn't know he had gone to see you until afterward.

Well, what did he tell you when he came back? That I had written some letter accusing one of your local hotshots of something? That maybe he was fooling around with my wife?

Did you write the letter, Mr. Chandler? she asked.

You're damn right I didn't write it, he shouted.

How did you know it was not handwritten? she asked.

Did I say that? he shouted. I couldn't have said that because how would I know? Whatever that kid told you was a lie.

Mr. Chandler, she said as she produced an official-looking paper from her desk, here is an affidavit, sworn to by Mr. Patrick Carroll before a local magistrate just last week. It says that, in his brief conversation with you, noting time and date, he asked if you knew that the letter had been confirmed as being in your handwriting and you said, and I quote from the affidavit, "…it was typed. I'm not that stupid…" and then you cursed him and threw him out.

She put the document down. Now, I've checked with the magistrate, and he is in his office two blocks away. You and I—she stood up—can go to his office now and you may swear, under oath, that Mr. Carroll is lying and that you did not say to him what his statement says you said. But you, being a man of business affairs, would know full well that the penalty for perjury in the state of Colorado is…let's see—she consulted a thick legal volume on her desk—two to eight with a half-million-dollar fine. Ready to go?

Now, just wait a minute, he said. I'm not getting involved in any "he said, I said" nonsense with some kid. I'm telling you I did not write that letter. He looked down. Even though I know full well this guy was fooling around with my wife. And if he got run out of town, as I heard, then he deserves what he got.

Mr. Chandler, she said evenly. It has been a busy period for magistrates around these parts this week. She tapped another official document. Your former wife has sworn, again under oath, that she did not have an affair or any intimate relations with Mr. Daniel Sheridan during a period from—she put on her glasses and consulted the document—the time you both arrived here in Durango and the time you personally left…rather abruptly, as I recall. What was all that about, I wonder?

Her lips were smiling, but her voice was icy. Now you have two statements you may swear to before the magistrate. That is, if you are inclined to do so.

Chandler's face was now so red she feared he might have a heart attack and collapse on her new carpet. Listen, he said, you print that kid's story, whatever he's made up, and say good-bye to your precious newspaper. I've consulted the best libel lawyers in Kansas City. In fact, they have prepared papers to get an injunction against this paper to prevent you from publishing his fictions.

Have they, now? she said, her smile still fixed. They clearly have consulted neither Colorado nor federal laws that will see their motion for an injunction in one door and out the other of any courtroom in America in less than five minutes. It's called "prior restraint," Mr. Chandler, and it violates the First Amendment to the Constitution of the United States of America. If you don't believe me, there is a Supreme Court case involving the government of the United States, in the form of President Richard Nixon as I recall, against *The New York Times* regarding publication of the Pentagon Papers. Mr. Nixon lost that one. And you'll lose yours. Now, I suggest in the interest of my time, if not also of yours, that we trot right down to the local magistrate so you can swear that Mr. Carroll and your former wife are lying—and you're not—or turn your legal eagles loose on me. Either way, I'll see you in court. It will be interesting at the very least. Perhaps even fun.

He started for the door and brushed copies of that day's *Herald* from her table. So be it, he said through gritted teeth. If that's the way you want it.

Just as he opened her office door, she said quietly, By the way, Mr. Chandler, what's all this about the arrangement your bank here made with the investment group… now let's see, what was it called?…something like Nature's

Capital, some years ago, just before you fled town or around that time?

He paused and turned. What about it? he said, now warily.

What about it is, as I understand it, that outfit invested heavily in your bank's stock and together you proposed a resource development fund to the Southern Utes that would have, had they agreed to it, turned over about ninety percent of any profits they received to you and that investment fund. And further, what about it is that the money the two tribal council members were alleged to have received from Mr. Sheridan actually came from you and Nature's Capital.

He came back into her office and said, Where did you get all this? This is confidential business information, and you or somebody has stolen private documents.

Mrs. Farnsworth said, I don't believe I claimed to have any documents. Though, as a matter of fact, I do. Not one of them is stolen. You've made a lot of people angry over the years, Mr. Chandler. Not just people in Durango, though God knows there were plenty of them. But other places as well. Some of those people, yes, with the help of your new friend Patrick Carroll, are now eager to settle scores. Mr. Carroll has enough information to write a fair-sized book on Russell Chandler, Nature's Capital, bribe offers, slander against Daniel Sheridan and, by the way, your wife—former wife—and the list of offenses gets pretty long.

He glared at her and threw up his hands. You dirty bitch, he muttered.

She smiled at him. Oh, Mr. Chandler. And here I thought you were a gentleman.

What next? he asked.

Here is my idea for what next, she said. Right next door is a stenographer. I thought about asking Patrick Carroll but didn't want you to be arrested for assault also. Anyway, you have a couple of hours before the next plane to Denver. So, why not just toddle next door and tell your story to the stenographer, every bit of it. And keep in mind, if you deviate one iota from the information contained in the documents we have with your name all over them, I promise you, you will see your false statement and those documents in the *Durango Herald* the next day, even if I have to put out a special edition. I suspect they also might be of interest to the *Kansas City Star* and, who knows, even the US Attorney in one of several states. The stenographer also happens to be a notary public. So, when you're finished with your story, she'll ask you to sign the paper, raise your hand, and swear it's the truth.

What's going to happen then? he asked. What do you intend to do with my statement?

I haven't decided, she said. My instincts are to put it in a safety deposit box and keep it as some kind of insurance against whatever further damage you try to do to friends of mine around here. On the other hand, you told some lies in this town, not only about Mr. Sheridan, but even about your own wife. I like them both, and that makes me kind of angry. Mr. Sheridan chose to remove himself from public service because of you and your treachery. It was a loss to this community and this state. He could have done some good. We'll never know now, will we? You can't go back and fix that up, even if you were man enough. And you're clearly not. So, I don't know.

She hesitated, then continued. Until a few days ago, I'd

probably have been satisfied just to have your statement in that box as insurance against further treachery. But I got a lecture recently from an honest and idealistic young man, one of the few left. He told me my business was not just to report the news and let the chips fall where they may. He told me that lies are cancers...to people and to nations. He told me newspapers weren't worth anything unless they revealed lies and liars and prevented them from becoming cancers.

I'll have to think about it. But in the meantime, Mr. Chandler, you are a liar, and Durango is better off without you.

She saw him clench his fist, and she smiled and said, Mr. Chandler, remember I'm just an elderly lady.

44.

She tethered her glossy filly on a long rope that would let her graze almost at will in the tall wild grass, then started to unpack her easel and paints. She hesitated and thought better of it.

Caroline took down the rolled blanket from behind the saddle and spread it in a shady spot at the edge of the grass. Sheridan may have his hidden lake, she thought, but I have this peaceful meadow almost always to myself. It was now mid-September and the golden aspen leaves were turning brown and falling. What a shame, she thought, that they couldn't stay shimmering gold year-round.

She drank cold white wine from the half-liter cooler and knew that the glorious summer days would soon give way to the winter. Already the nights were cool enough for blankets at her place near 8,000 feet. September had become her favorite month of the year for its fading splendor, fall hues, and the closing down of nature for its winter sleep.

Daniel Sheridan was never far from her mind. Throughout the day, she found herself wondering, without prompting, where he was and what he was doing. He would be looking after his cattle, checking for hoof and mouth, putting in hay for the winter, making sure the spring calves weren't taking too long to wean. He took his cattle ranching seriously, as he did much else. But not always. She thought of his dreaded water finortens and laughed out loud.

Sometimes he seemed like a boy to her, obvious and transparent, easy to read and understand. At other times, though, he was self-contained, almost remote. She never knew where he was during those times, what he was thinking, what caused his mind, maybe even his heart, to move away somewhere. She did not know where. She could not decide whether she would like him to be always one predictable thing or whether his facets and shades in fact made him more intriguing.

Her mind drifted back to the time when she first arrived in Durango and began to move about, to socialize, and to look for ways to take part in the community. She shook her head remembering Sheridan the county commissioner, the man who some thought might be, ought to be, governor. He was at ease on his feet and in managing the commission. He was confident without being, as some men are, self-promoting and aggressive. She marveled then and now at how he projected strength without making the least effort to do so. It was simply who he was.

Caroline on occasion wondered whether she was in love with him, and on this occasion she did so. She supposed she was. Though after her disastrous misjudgment of Russell Chandler, she was never quite sure how much to trust her own emotions. Live and learn. Given a chance, over time, would I learn that I had misjudged Sheridan also? she pondered. How can we ever know? She supposed she would like to have the chance to find out.

She consciously avoided thoughts of marriage. What complications it held. She could not see them living together constantly. What if we were to get married? she thought. He would keep his place, and I would keep mine. We would have separate bedrooms, she thought, but when together we would always sleep in the same bed. She loved the feel of that strong arm around her when she was awakened in the night.

But she knew he would always want the freedom to slip away, to go to his hidden lake, to camp out by himself, to feel the wilderness, to confront the cougar. Alright, she thought to herself, I can handle that. It is who he is.

His reliance on the Ute holy man thrilled her in a way. It showed a spiritual side few men she knew had ever revealed. Whatever it was, it was a lot more profound than church every Sunday. And it wasn't about life hereafter. It was about life here and now, a life inseparable from the natural world. That was it, she thought. That is what makes Daniel Sheridan unlike others she had known. He relies on that holy man to help keep him connected to what he knows to be real.

She simply could not see Sheridan in a city or driving a big car or buying expensive clothes. She knew for a fact that he had one worn western sport jacket, with leather patched elbows, and an equally worn pair of slacks he wore with it. That was it. She had never seen him in a white shirt or suit. A long way from Wall Street, she thought. But a good long way.

Most of her life had been spent planning ahead, making budgets, calculating interest rates on savings and the growth of stocks, thinking about next year. She suddenly realized she had done none of that since Russell left. And since her friendship with Sheridan, she realized she was adopting his outlook and his life values. Worse things, she knew, could have happened to her.

Durango was Caroline's home. She never intended to leave it. And she assumed Sheridan would always be there.

45.

They sat on her porch at sunset. She knew the evening was going to be different when he set a bottle of tequila on the small table between them. This is to get your way of thinking together with my way of thinking, he said with a laugh.

It burned her throat and she suppressed a cough. He laughed again. Get used to it, he said. Can't drink the Jameson all the time.

And why exactly should I get used to it? she asked. Is this a signal you've switched drinks and therefore I have to as well, after I've taken all these years to get used to Irish?

No, he said, this tequila merely signals that I've got a plan.

How much of this stuff do I have to drink before I know what it is?

Ha, he snorted. Another sip or two will just about get you in the mood. Here's my idea. When the snow gets deep, say just after Christmas, let's go down to Mexico. One of those places with warm sands and blue water. He leaned back in his chair and said, What do you think?

Come to think of it, I've never been to Mexico, she said lightheartedly. It would be an adventure.

Alright, he said smacking his hand on the table, that's it then. I'll get Harv Waldron's son to look in on the cattle and take care of Toby and Red. January the big snows will set in here and while all our friends and neighbors are freezing their butts, we'll be down south drinking this stuff—he gestured at the tequila—getting sunburned on the beach, and eating the best enchiladas in the world. How about it?

Well, sure, she said. Why not? But are you certain you want to do something really crazy like leave Durango, leave Colorado, go to a foreign country? She said "foreign" in a way that made it sound like Mars.

Look here, missy, he said, you may think I'm nothing but a broken-down old cowpoke. But a while back, in my youth, I was in the Marines and I saw a good bit of the world. I've been around. I can handle myself. You may have to help me count the change down there, but I can take care of most of the rest of it. So, what do you say?

I say yes, she answered. You planning to stay a month or two, or what exactly did you have in mind?

Nothing like that, he said. I figure a week or so is about all I can be gone. He took a swallow of tequila. But you never know. We could get down there and a great blizzard could hit this place. Close the airport and we might even have to stay a few extra days till they got things dug out up here.

Well, that answers one question, she said. We'll fly down and back. I was afraid you might propose horseback all the way.

Ha, he laughed. That would be something, wouldn't it? Just like the old days. Too far for Red, though. He's a trail horse, not a highway horse.

Let's see, she said counting on her fingers. January gives me about four months to get into shape to wear the swimsuit that I haven't worn for about five years.

Sheridan waved his hand, enjoying the thought. I wouldn't worry about a thing like that if I were you. I plan on finding a little private beach of our own and just go kinda natural. That'd be okay, wouldn't it? Besides, I haven't owned a bathing suit for longer than I can remember.

If you don't mind, I'm going to start out with my swimsuit, at least until I get used to going without it.

Why, missy, as I recall, I saw most of what there was to see up there at my lake a couple of weeks ago. Is there something else you've got to hide?

Don't be cute, she smacked his arm. It's just a woman's instinctive modesty. You men ought to take it up some day.

Oh, I'm about the most modest man you ever met, Sheridan said. And I've got a lot to be modest about.

I think it will be grand, she said and leaned in to kiss him. Let's go. Can't wait until January. The sun about then will feel really good. But you do have to promise me one thing.

What's that? he asked.

No finortens.

Oh, yes ma'am, he said, laughing. No finortens. But…
they do have some sharks.

46.

Frances Farnsworth took several days to decide whether to
tell Caroline about her former husband's confrontational
visit. In the end she knew she had no choice. It was a small
town, and even airport and taxi people, besides those at the
Herald, might spread the word. Caroline would be upset
not to know. And Sheridan ought to be there as well. His
life had been even more dislodged by Russell Chandler's
manipulations. She sighed and thought, That complete
nightmare of a human being was still capable of further
mischief, sworn statement or not.

Daniel and Caroline came for drinks the next Friday
evening. There has been some activity around here in the
past few days that affects you both, Frances began. She
then recounted in considerable detail Russell Chandler's
assault on her office and the Patrick Carroll revelations that
led up to it. Then she waited.

Sheridan looked out her large east window in silence.
Caroline said, That bastard. That loathsome bastard.

Sheridan remained silent, though his face was clouded.

Frances gestured toward two file folders on the reading table next to her chair. I have a set of documents for
you both if you'd like them. It is Patrick Carroll's complete
story, starting fifteen years ago and working up to today.
And a copy of Mr. Chandler's statement he left with us.

Sheridan shook his head in the negative. Frances handed Caroline a folder and said, He hedged a good deal in his statement, but I must say he was much more candid than I expected. I surely must have put the fear of God in him.

Caroline said, What are you going to do? If you print all of this—or even part of it—I'm afraid I will not want to be around here for awhile.

Frances said, Mr. Sheridan, what about you?

I'd just as soon you left me—us—alone, he said. This doesn't change anything. It's ancient history. It just rakes up old dirt. I don't see as how it does anybody any good. Might sell a few newspapers. But then what? You'd have all the town gossips going back over it all and it would be the bad old days all over again. I learned a long time ago that if people wanted to think the worst of you they would do so whatever the facts were. What's done is done, at least where I'm concerned.

What about Caroline? Frances asked him. Wouldn't you like to see her reputation restored?

Sheridan grimaced. There's nothing wrong with her reputation and it doesn't need restoring. But that's for her to say. If that's what she wants, of course I'll stay out of the way.

The wounds that were caused are now old, Caroline said. I don't see them being healed by reopening them, Frances. Besides, this is not our decision. You're the newspaper woman. This is your information and you can, and probably will, do with it as you please.

Frances said, I wouldn't hurt you, my dear friend, for all the newsprint in the world. But I did give your former husband a lecture that was recently given to me. It was about suppressing lies. Learning to live with them. And the consequences that causes for years thereafter. What do you do—what do I do—when I know a serious wrong has been done and it should be made right, but to make it right involves bringing further misery...reopening old wounds? She shook her head. I don't know the answer to that. I wish I did.

No one cares now, Sheridan said.

They should, Frances said with considerable heat. *They should*. I know for a fact that people, good people, stayed away from local government because of what happened to you. All of a sudden, because of the treachery of this awful man, civic duty was tarnished. Politics and government were tainted. Good people didn't want to touch them.

Sheridan shrugged. So be it. If people suddenly believe bad things about someone they've known for a long time... if they gossiped and dragged this fine woman—he gestured at Caroline—in the dirt, that's their fault.

Alright, Frances said, I will be brutally honest. This has been on my conscience all these years. Back then, the *Herald* covered the story as if it were a sports event. We printed the outrageously false accusations, even though they were anonymous, because if we hadn't we'd have been accused of a cover-up. We printed your denial, when you stepped down...or stepped away. It was a sensational political story, at least by local standards, and we helped make it a statewide story. I'm ashamed of that, and now I have a chance to set it right.

It sounds to me like you promised Russell you wouldn't, Caroline said.

Frances said, I didn't promise him anything. I said I'd have to think about it. I wanted him to have this hanging over his head for the rest of his life. I wanted that threat to keep him awake at night. I wanted him at least to get an ulcer, if not also a heart attack.

Well, I've said my piece, Sheridan said and stood up. I'll thank you for the drink and bid you ladies good night. As far as I'm concerned, Caroline has my vote. I'll leave it to the both of you to decide about this. Right now I'm mostly interested in getting this new Animas–La Plata project brass bound and copper riveted before things fall apart again. In the grand scheme of things, it's more important that this town get itself back together and move on than anything that might happen to me, one way or the other.

He bent to kiss Caroline and murmured in her ear, then shook Frances's hand and left.

After he was gone, Caroline said, What do we do with a man like that?

Mrs. Farnsworth said, If it were up to me, I'd put his statue in the courthouse square.

47.

It's done, Leonard Cloud said. He and Sam Maynard had just returned from three days in Washington. They were reporting to an informal meeting of the Southern Ute tribal council.

Sam Maynard said, He will not like me saying this, but Mr. Cloud deserves a medal. You would all be proud of what your chairman did in Washington. We met with the chairman of the Senate appropriations committee, who said the first year of construction money for Animas–La Plata will be in the next federal budget. That was confirmed by the secretary of the Interior and the director of the Bureau of Reclamation. They all showed us the papers that guaranteed it.

He grinned widely, and the council stood and applauded them both.

Leonard Cloud said quietly, It has been a very long road for our people. But we are now almost to the end. We will start digging the Ridges Basin Dam in the spring. In fact, the people we met in Washington said it would be perfectly fitting to have a ground-breaking ceremony this fall as a celebration.

There was much laughter and backslapping around the council table.

Leonard Cloud opened large spreadsheets and said, We will pass these around so that you can all see them. These are timelines that plot out the progress of the project. The most important thing is that the pipeline from the reservoir to the reservation will be opened, according to this plan, two years from next spring when the reservoir is filled. In the meantime, we can go ahead now and begin to make contracts between Red Willow and energy development companies.

Sam Maynard said, My firm—your law firm—has already begun to draft contracts between Red Willow and investors willing to finance your development projects here and between Red Willow and those energy companies.

Leonard Cloud said, This council agreed unanimously a long time ago to three things. First, all of these contracts will be made available to all tribal members and to the public at large. And second, every bit of energy development we undertake will be according to the strictest standards of environmental protection. The final thing is that a large percentage of proceeds from our energy resources will be placed in the Southern Ute Tribal Trust Fund for the use of our children and their children.

We are preparing requests for proposals for the council's approval, Maynard said, to issue to Colorado and national environmental consulting firms for a competition to select one or more companies who will guarantee these standards are met at every step.

The tribal secretary asked, When can we have the ground-breaking? Let's do it as soon as possible.

Leonard Cloud said, We'll have to consult with the mayor of Durango and the La Plata county commissioners. And we want to issue a press release inviting everyone from the community to attend. But Mr. Maynard and I discussed on the plane yesterday the idea of having it a week from Saturday, probably in the morning, and having some shovels for the digging and a platform for all the speeches at the site where the Ridges Basin Dam will be just south of town.

Sam Maynard said, Mr. Cloud and I calculated that the weather has been known to move in on us in a surprising way in late September, early October. So we want to do it soon. And before those politicians in Washington change their minds.

They all laughed.

48.

It was glorious, Sam said. I brought Mr. Cloud with me so he can tell you I'm not just blowing smoke signals, so to speak.

Mr. Murphy said, I can't believe that for once those clowns in Washington did the right thing.

Tom, Sam said, they didn't have a choice. We've been kicking this project down the road for over thirty years and not a drop of Animas water yet sits in storage. We finally came along with a deal they couldn't refuse. Mr. Cloud signed off for the Utes and we had letters of intent from the city of Durango and the county of La Plata. We even had two senators and a guy from the governor's office with us. For all practical purposes, we had everybody that mattered there to cheer us on.

Leonard Cloud said, Gentlemen, don't forget that this gets rid of a big thorn in the government's side. They've had to deal with this—up and down, back and forth— for a long time. They were just waiting for all of us to get together. When the Interior Department people and the senators heard that the Indians wanted this done this way, they couldn't have been happier.

Bill Van Ness said, Sammy was telling us you had some other folks there on your side.

Sure did, Sam Maynard said. Mr. Cloud's counterpart from the Navajo Nation joined us and brought the New Mexico congressional delegation along. The only thing we didn't do was put the chiefs in native costume and have them do a little victory dance.

Leonard Cloud smiled in spite of himself. What those folks liked mostly, he said, was that this satisfies the Indian water claims and gets those out of the way without more lawsuits. And the project is smaller and costs less than it was originally designed to. Given today's federal budgets, this little dam is a pretty inexpensive way to get the Indians off their back.

Well, hallelujah, Mr. Murphy said. That's a first for Washington. Something smaller and cheaper. Even I'd vote for that.

The professor said, The main thing is that this town now has a chance to get this cocklebur out from under its saddle and move on. There hasn't been anything in this town's long history that caused more confusion and more bad feelings that the Animas–La Plata. A lot of us never liked it and just wished it would go away. But when it became a Ute water project, that made it a lot more palatable.

Water is water, dams are dams, Professor, Mr. Murphy said huffily. How come this one becomes okay when Mr. Cloud's people—with all due respect—get the water, and not the people of Durango?

The difference, Tom, is that the Utes have been denied their water rights for a century and the original project was going to put a lot more dollars in the hands of some fat-cat develops and mining moguls.

Sam said, Now, folks, we just got this thing wrapped up. We're all laying down our cudgels and the lion will lay down with the lamb. A new day has arrived and we're all going to enjoy this coffee on a remarkable day in paradise and not look back.

As the Monday and Friday coffee club broke up and drifted away, Leonard Cloud put his hand on Sam Maynard's arm and said, Sam, I know you've begun to put this ground-breaking ceremony together for next week. And I just want to say that there's one person who has to be there. It's Danny Sheridan. We wouldn't be doing this now if he hadn't got together with us down in Ignacio and come up with a water allocation formula that made sense to the tribes and could be sold to the leaders here in town and in Washington. He deserves the credit and he's got to be there.

Sam studied his friend's face, then looked away. Mr. Cloud, he won't come. He won't come for a lot of reasons. He's a private man. He doesn't like noise and big gatherings and speeches and bands and all that. It's just not his kind of thing, and it never was.

It isn't fair, Leonard Cloud said.

Of course it isn't, Sam said, and you more than anyone are a judge of what's fair and what's not. But what isn't fair is what happened years ago, and it had to do with the Utes and the project, and while he put all that behind him a long time ago, it still has to have put a fishhook in his heart.

I'd feel better if we at least tried, Leonard Cloud said.

Tell you what I'll do, Sam responded. There is only one person who could convince him and that's Caroline Chandler. I'll have a word with her and see if she can persuade him.

49.

Did you do this, Mr. Carroll? Frances's face looked to the young reporter like the wrath of God.

Do what? Patrick asked. Do what?

There are only three copies of your story and one other document, and they are all in my safe at the paper, she said. You have the finished draft of your story and all your notes and research. No one else has anything—at least to my knowledge. Did you give them to anyone? Did you discuss this with anyone? Have you been in touch with any other news organization? And I beg of you, for the sake of your own future, do not lie to me.

Patrick looked pale. No, ma'am, I swear it. No. I haven't. I wouldn't. This story belongs to the *Durango Herald*. I wrote it on your time and your money. Except the trip to Kansas City. I paid for that.

Very well, she said. If at any point you wish to change your story, in your own interest you better do so.

Why are you asking me this? he said.

I'm asking you this because an hour ago, for the first time in my very long professional life, I got a call from a newspaper asking for a comment. The paper is the *Rocky Mountain News*, and it was the managing editor in Denver.

Comment on what? Patrick said.

On your story, Mr. Carroll. That's why I'm questioning you. How did they get your story? Even worse, I think they might run it.

The young man was standing in Frances's office holding tightly to the back of a chair facing her large desk. I don't know, he said. I can't imagine. I didn't talk to anyone about it. I wouldn't have...

What's the matter? she said. What just occurred to you?

He hesitated. What just occurred to me is my friend Mitch. He was my roommate at Fort Lewis. He's the guy who tracked Chandler down, in the very city where he works.

Does he have the story? she demanded.

No, he doesn't have the whole story. I never showed it to him after I wrote it. But he does know about Chandler. He does know why I was looking for him. I had to tell him the background. And all that's a matter of public record anyway. Let me call him and see if he knows anything about this.

You do that, Mr. Carroll, she said. Then you come right back in here and talk to me.

Patrick went into his office and dialed his friend in Kansas City. Mitch, for God's sake, have you talked to anyone about Russell Chandler? Have you shared any of the information we've been working on?

Of course not, Pat, Mitch said. Why would I do a thing like that? But listen to this, a couple of my colleagues here at our investigating company had to know what I was up to and it turns out the knives are out for this guy at least as much here as down there where you are.

About what? Carroll asked.

About his investment bank taking a lot of people to the cleaners, including a couple of the principals of my own company, on some kind of fast-buck derivative scheme. They collected big fees and the deal went south.

But Mitch, my boss is about to can me because somehow my story got out and another paper has it.

What other paper? Mitch said.

The *Rocky Mountain News*, Carroll said.

Wait a minute, Mitch said. Now this rings a bell. A guy down the hall helped me out with this case—your case—and he's got a girlfriend who's a reporter for that paper. Let me think about this. I had to tell him what was up to get his help doing some complicated financial tracking of our quarry. He's the guy who actually found Chandler here in town. I'll check with him, but it's within the realm of reason that he might have found this case interesting enough, particularly with Chandler's Colorado connections, to pass it on to his girlfriend. Get some brownie points, you might say. Come to think of it, that's got to be what happened.

Mitch, my notes, the draft of my story, all those papers, Carroll said. You didn't show them to him, did you?

Patrick, my friend, of course I did, Mitch said. He had to know what was going down to do his job, to help us out.

Mitch, is it possible he might have copied all that stuff and sent it to his girlfriend? Carroll asked in anguish.

In the dirty business of life, Mitch said, it is not only possible, I would have to say it is more than probable. Sorry, pal. If you get sacked, let me know. Maybe you can come work for us.

Patrick Carroll tapped lightly on Mrs. Farnsworth's door. Come in, she commanded. He told her about his conversation with Mitch. She said, I see. Alright, I want you to get in touch with this reporter in Denver. Appeal to her sense of journalistic collegiality, if she has any, and see what the *Rocky*'s plans are. She will probably ask what our plans are, and you say that I haven't decided yet. That some unfairly damaged reputations are in jeopardy of further damage. Chances are she will scoff at that and say something like "news is news." The *Rocky* will now think it owns the story and will not want to be scooped by us. Tell her we'll let her know in the next forty-eight hours and ask that they give us that time. I need to make a couple of phone calls.

50.

I've given it considerable thought, Sheridan said, and I've talked to Sammy about it, and I just don't think I'd feel comfortable there.

He was sitting at Caroline's kitchen table on Friday morning. She said, That's certainly understandable. All those folks, particularly Leonard and the Southern Utes, will be disappointed. But they have to understand.

What about you? he asked. Are you going down tomorrow morning?

I don't know yet, she said. I'm still trying to decide. It would be easier if you were going. But it is a historic moment for this place, for sure.

Caroline paused, then said, I got a call from Frances yesterday. She was very upset. It seems that, through some kind of comedy of errors, one of the Denver papers got Patrick Carroll's story about Russell, and she thinks they might run it. She was beside herself. I've never heard her so upset.

That's too bad, Sheridan said. I was kinda hoping she would keep it locked up and maybe the whole thing would go away.

That's what she wanted, I believe, Caroline said. But once it fell into the other paper's hands, it was out of her control. I guess at least for some people it's too juicy to pass up.

It's a strange world, missy, Sheridan said, one I still can't quite get used to. Nobody's got any privacy anymore. Everybody's business is everybody's business now. You'd think in a place like Durango that world would pass us by and leave us alone. But I guess it's too much to hope for.

GARY HART

I know, Daniel, it isn't fair. But I think the good news is that when everybody's business is everybody's business, maybe it goes away quicker. There is too much sensationalism and scandal to keep up with and pretty soon people either drown in it or go mad or just shrug it off. Mostly the latter, I think. If everything's a scandal, then nothing is a scandal. Most overused word in modern America.

He drank his coffee and thought. Well, if those Denver newspaper folks were to ask my opinion, and for all I know they'll try, I'd just tell 'em to publish and be damned. Nothing I can do about it anyway. He took her hand. But I'd just as soon they left you alone. You've suffered enough because of me.

No, Daniel, don't say that. You haven't caused me any suffering, she said, quite the contrary. You and your way of life, Red and Toby, your ranch, your lake, your cougar—she laughed—even your damned finortens, are a blessing to me. I've never been happier and more contented in my life.

Well, then, he said, I tell you what. Come up to the place tonight and I'll cook up two of the biggest, most beautiful trout you ever saw. Brought them down the last time I was in the high country. I went downtown to the bookstore yesterday and got some maps and travel stuff about Mexico, and we'll finish off that tequila and plan our trip. What do you say?

I say that would be perfect, Caroline said. I had planned to bake a chocolate pie today. Would it be okay if I brought it along? You do like chocolate, don't you?

Hate it, he said. You'd better bring two.

51.

At the site of the proposed Ridges Basin Dam, several miles south of Durango toward the boundary of the Southern Ute reservation, the Durango High School band was warming up its repertoire of Souza marches for the big groundbreaking ceremony the following morning.

A makeshift speaking platform for the dignitaries was being hammered together. Every half hour or so, a city official showed up to order it extended a few more feet. By now the attendee list included both US senators from Colorado, the Fourth District congressman, the mayor and city council of Durango, the La Plata County Commission, the chairmen of the Southern Ute and Ute Mountain Ute Tribes, the deputy director of the Bureau of Reclamation and a special assistant to the Secretary of the Interior from Washington, and a passel of water big shots from Denver.

The mayor of Durango had assumed the position of master of ceremonies and was agonizing about the number and length of the speeches. The politicians would, of course, each have to speak. But they were all politicians.

Behind the scenes, the real organization was being carried out by Sam Maynard, who had issued most of the invitations and followed up to insure attendance of the most important figures. It had not been difficult. He kept repeating the Kennedy saying about victory having a thousand fathers and laughed every time he did.

Sam Maynard had called Dan Sheridan the day before. He said, It would be great if you'd be here for this, Dan.

Sheridan had demurred, talked about a couple of calves that were sickly, and mentioned the forecast of a storm in the high country.

Sam said, I've been checking with the weather service about every hour. You're right about the high country, up in the Weminuche and the Needles, but it's supposed to keep north and east of Durango. We're supposed to have sunshine, at least in the morning, so I think it'll be okay. I hope you'll think about being here.

Well, Sam, Sheridan said, I do appreciate it. And I'll give it some thought. But if I do get down there, we got to have an understanding. No platform, no introduction, no speech. You may just see me toward the back of the crowd. I'll be the tall, ugly guy. Arrive late and leave early.

Better than nothing, Daniel, Sam said. Though my sense of justice tells me we ought to hang a big medal around your neck for this. And Mr. Cloud agrees.

You try to hang a medal around my neck anytime soon, Mr. Maynard, Sheridan said, and I'll hang something a lot less pleasant around yours.

Sam laughed and said, See you tomorrow. He stayed an hour or two longer to supervise the location of the Stars and Stripes and the blue and white Colorado flag with the big red and yellow *C* in the middle. And he watched as the red, white, and blue bunting was strung around the platform and speakers' stand.

Then Sam Maynard returned to his office to complete his list of calls and confirmations. He had worked on this project nearly all of his life. Throughout those thirty-some years, he had often thought it would never happen, that it was a pipe dream, that his beloved Utes would never get their water, in more recent times that hotheads in Durango might take to shooting it out. But here it was, and he found it difficult to believe. Tomorrow morning shovels were actually going to be put into the earth. Dirt would be moved along the banks of the Animas. He slapped his desk in happiness and said to himself, By God, this is actually—finally—going to happen.

52.

Frances Farnsworth hung up the phone and began to type on her computer. She was writing an editorial, two editorials, for the morning paper. The first was a celebration of the commencement of the Animas–La Plata water project so important to southwestern Colorado. The second was a commentary on the Russell Chandler story that she had just been told by the managing editor of the *Rocky Mountain News* would run in its Sunday edition.

She completed the first, then picked up the phone. Caroline, she said, I'm calling to say that the Denver paper will have much, though not all, of the exposé on your former husband and his serpentine manipulations down here years ago. And apparently he's got himself in more financial hot water where he is now. The Denver paper is using the Colorado connection to anchor the longer story about financial mismanagement in high places. I'm writing an editorial for tomorrow that tries to put all this into some sort of historical—and, yes, moral—context. I have no choice but to let people around here know what's coming.

It can't be stopped? Caroline asked with heavy resignation.

Afraid not, my dear, Frances said. I'm not going to run the full story or even part of it. I'd already decided that. But the workings of my profession once more took charge of fortune and fate. The story will be out. It's messy stuff, especially since it involves your former husband. But the good news—as we occasionally say around here—is that it will make Daniel Sheridan look like a redeemed hero and the longtime victim of a real serpent.

I needn't tell you that he will like neither part of that, Caroline said. He's made it clear since all this came up that he's not anyone's victim and he doesn't need restoration.

This isn't for him, Frances said. It's for us. For Durango. It was a lie, and it has been a cancer in this community. And it did have to be dug out for the sake of everyone's future. I didn't want young Carroll to stir up this pot at the beginning. But he convinced me that it had to be done. And now, despite Daniel's uneasiness with the spotlight once again, it is the absolute best thing for Durango. I'm just glad I didn't end up having to do it—for the very reasons you've stated.

He will have to bear with it, Caroline said. And if anyone can, he can. He's the strongest man I've ever met. I'm seeing him tonight. Let me tell him what's going to happen.

Thank you for doing that, Frances said. I was not looking forward to the call. Do you think you can persuade him to come to the ground breaking tomorrow?

I might have before, Caroline said, but I seriously doubt it now. The *Rocky* will not be out until Sunday. But I gather you want your editorial out tomorrow.

Frances said, I do. The only way I can preempt the *Rocky* and forewarn everyone is to run the piece tomorrow.

Caroline said, I'll explain all this to Dan. He hasn't told you, but you must know how much he appreciates your understanding about all this.

I do know it, Frances said. But it is not his style to say so. She hesitated, then said, Do me a favor this evening. Maybe after your first drink. Say to him that he is a hero and he always will be so long as any of us are alive to remember his service to Durango and this area. But most of all he is a hero for holding his head up under very bad circumstances and for teaching all of us what character really is.

53.

The phone rang and Sheridan picked it up. Dan, it's Steve Ramsey. I hate to do this to you yet again. But we're putting some search parties together to bring down some kids from the Weminuche and I'm wondering if one of the teams could use your place again as a collection point?

Of course, Sheriff, Sheridan said, you're always welcome. Tell me what's going on.

Pretty much the usual, the sheriff said. Three kids from the college—new ones this year, I guess—got it in their heads to camp out in the high country and as usual didn't pay much attention to the weather. The weather service is forecasting the first big storm tonight and the people at Fort Lewis and their friends are scared these kids will get caught in it and get frozen.

It'd help to have an idea of where they might have got themselves to, Sheridan said.

We're pretty sure it's up near the Vallecito Basin. There's a trail along Johnson Creek up there, and they told their friends they were going to camp out at Columbine Lake, just west and a little south of Mount Hope.

I know it, Sheridan said. Who's coming up here?

A couple of my guys, a couple of US Forest Service rangers who know the area, and one or two of the local mountain rescue types. Another group is forming up at the north end of Vallecito Reservoir and will head north up that trail and come into the area from the east. And we've got a third group coming over from Pagosa Springs. They can use those four-wheelers part of the way after they leave their trucks.

You got an army, Sheriff, Sheridan said. Just make sure your guys don't get themselves lost.

Naw, the sheriff said, this is the A team. You know most of them. Seems one of the girls is some big shot's daughter. So, I wasn't given any choice but to roll out the best. And the group coming to your place should be there in about fifteen minutes. They'll need to park their horse trailers at your place, if you don't mind.

Don't mind at all. Problem is, Sheridan said, looking at his watch, it's going to take a good three or four hours or more to get up there on horseback. And if that weather comes in, it could get pretty shaky getting down from up there. Might have to overnight. I hope your guys have their long johns and sleeping bags.

They do, the sheriff said, though if we're lucky and those kids are where they're supposed to be, it's not out of the question everybody can get back by midnight. We've got a chopper coming down from Grand Junction to try to locate these kids from the air while it's still daylight and make sure they're alright. If we could find a clearing up there, we might even try to lift them out.

Not much clearing around that area, Sheridan said, and a lot of tall trees and some pretty steep slopes. I probably know that area better than any of your guys. You want me to take them up there?

Naw, Dan, you don't have to do that. We've rousted you out much too often. Just give our guys some guidance and go over their maps with them so they know what they're doing. Then he hung up.

When the rangers, deputies, and rescue crew arrived, they parked their trucks and horse trailers, unloaded their horses, and saddled up. Sheridan bent over their trail maps on his kitchen table, pointing out trails, gulches, streams, and rough patches, and suggested the most effective route up and back. Once found, the students would have to leave their gear and double up on the horses of their rescuers to get down. Sheridan made the crew check their heavy-duty flashlights. It's either going to be overnight up there or a long dark ride down to get back here by midnight, he said.

Sheridan watched as they assembled in his yard. He then made a quick decision, scribbled a note and placed it against a brown paper–wrapped package on his table. He patted Toby and told him to watch the house.

He went to the barn and saddled Red. He put on a parka and a liner with ear covers under his Stetson. Out in the yard he told the group that he would take them up as far as he could to make sure they found their way. Despite their disavowals of his obligation, he said, I can get you up there faster than you can get yourselves there. We don't have a lot of time to waste.

He led them across the north end of the Waldron property to the east and then north up the McClure Canyon toward the Endlich Mesa. A trail there would take them due north past Lake Marie and up the Crystal Valley toward Columbine Pass and Columbine Lake. They would pass just west of Sheridan Mountain, the 13,000-foot peak his grandfather had climbed and given his name in 1906.

54.

The lights were on when Caroline reached the Sheridan ranch that evening. She knocked repeatedly, with Toby jumping and barking inside the door, until she finally found it open and went in. She couldn't account for the yard full of trailers and trucks, but assumed it was one of the rescue parties Sheridan had told her about.

Her calls to Daniel went unanswered, and she asked Toby for his whereabouts as if she expected an answer. She thought he must have needed a last-minute dinner item and had gone to the tiny grocery and tavern down the road. She must have just missed him.

Then she saw the package and note on the table. The note said, "Have gone up to find some stray lambs. Fix your dinner and leave some in the frig for me. Don't drink all the tequila. Will be back late. Dan." Then she saw something he had never written to her before scrawled at the bottom. "I love you."

She didn't like this at all. *He shouldn't keep tempting fate like this*, she thought. *Why can't he just...settle down?*

she thought. Then the idea made her laugh and she relaxed. He couldn't do those things, she realized, because if he did he wouldn't be Dan Sheridan.

She drank a little tequila, and it burned fiercely. She got crackers and cheese to lessen the fire and ate them with the drink until she relaxed. She looked at her watch as the sun began to sink. How far up? Where did he have to go? She knew from the yard full of trailers and trucks that he was not alone. In fact, he was leading a cavalry unit, she thought. At least he wasn't up there by himself.

She sighed and settled in for a long, and mostly lonely, evening. Toby followed her everywhere and stayed close to her when she sat down. She turned on Sheridan's radio for news and music. After an hour or so, a weather bulletin warned about heavy snow and high winds in the high country. And she did not like that information. The early winter storm was coming down from Montana through western Colorado and on to the southeast. It was expected to bring heavy drifts in the San Juan Mountains but bypass the city of Durango.

Thinking that by some miracle he might be back earlier in the evening, she considered it best to cook the trout she found in the refrigerator and have it, together with some corn, ready for a late supper. He would be hungry. But he would also be thirsty. She poured another bit of tequila but made sure they was plenty left for him. She occupied some time looking at the maps and reading the tourist booklets laid out on the kitchen table and planning a getaway to a Cabo San Lucas beach when the January weather came.

Once she had rolled the fish in cornmeal and fried it the way he had shown her, she found it difficult to eat very much. She had little appetite and considered that she probably would not until he got back safe and sound.

From time to time, Toby would go to the kitchen door, look toward the barn, and whine softly. She called him back to the kitchen table and gave him bites of her fish.

She thought of the unopened package on the front room table and brought it into the kitchen. She untied the string and unwrapped the paper. It was the carved figure of an Indian woman holding a bird, perhaps a dove, in her arms. She wore a traditional dress that fell almost to her feet. The figure was long and sinuous. It had been freshly oiled and rubbed, and the walnut glistened. She read and reread the note he had left.

For a time she held the figure so tight her knuckles turned white. She sent up a silent prayer. She didn't know what else to do. Very late that evening she lay down on the worn leather living room sofa and covered herself with a sheepskin throw. She thought it best to wait for Sheridan like this. It would do little good to continue to stand by the window hour after hour.

Despite her vow to await his arrival, she presently fell into a deep sleep. Toby lay on the floor close beside her.

55.

At ten o'clock that Saturday morning, the dignitaries filed onto the platform at the Ridges Basin Dam site. A crowd of close to two thousand had gathered, much to Sam Maynard's delight. He scanned the back of the crowd for Daniel

Sheridan's familiar hat but could not locate it. He somehow felt Sheridan would come late, but he would be there.

The band played "The Star-Spangled Banner" and the crowd sang along. The opening remarks were delivered by the mayor and then by his predecessor, old Mayor Hurley. The speeches then began and ran on for quite a while.

Despite instructions for brief remarks, too many on the platform saw an opportunity to claim credit, to compliment each other, or to view with delight the dawn of a wonderful new day. And this day turned out to be a brilliant fall Colorado day. Despite the storm clouds moving out of the San Juans and drifting to the southeast, the sun shone and the day began to turn warm.

After well over an hour of talks, the principals came off the platform and filed to the nearby beribboned dam site. Shiny new shovels were handed out and, predictably, there were not enough to go around. Several political figures ended up sharing grips with other political figures, some sworn enemies. But it was too important a day for old grievances and grudges.

After the shovels were turned and the ribbon ceremoniously cut, the crowd began to disperse and the dignitaries went to their cars to drive north to the Durango City Hall for a celebratory lunch.

Those who had not found that morning's *Durango Herald* on their doorstep had heard of a significant editorial on the front page, and they stopped at newsstands and drugstores to get a copy. Soon small groups of people in restaurants and coffee shops and even on street corners were reading the editorial and exchanging surprised comments. Here's what they read:

A Time for Justice and for Healing

Most citizens of Durango will remember a time twelve years ago when accusations anonymously circulated against one of our leading citizens. That citizen, then chairman of the La Plata County Commission, resigned his position and retired from a public life that some, perhaps many, hoped might lead to the governorship of Colorado.

Tomorrow a Colorado newspaper will publish a story documenting how the allegations against this gentleman were false, and it will attribute them to a former businessman in Durango named Russell Chandler. Mr. Chandler recently admitted to the publisher of this newspaper in a sworn statement that he was the author of the false accusations knowing them to be false. He further admits that the charges of corruption rendered against that public official, Daniel Sheridan, were not only false but were made both to discredit Mr. Sheridan and to conceal that it was Mr. Chandler himself who was guilty of fraud, bribery, and corruption.

Tomorrow everyone in this community will be able to read the details of this sordid business, and they should know that a good man, and a good woman, were wronged in a terrible fashion. For this, this newspaper bears its share of blame for following the story without due diligence to the facts and without insisting on more than rumor and speculation. We admit our error and ask the community, and particularly Mr. Sheridan, for forgiveness. Quality journalism, protected by the Constitution, should never let this happen.

When all this quiets down, and we hope it will soon, each of us might look into our own souls and ask how often we have contributed to, or perhaps merely condoned, the casual character destruction that has become a hallmark of our public life. In that process, we encourage as many citizens of Durango as feel so moved to join us in apologizing to Daniel Sheridan and asking for his forgiveness. He is the very best that this fine city has to offer.

Frances Farnsworth
Publisher

56.

Deep in troubled dreams at the very break of dawn, Caroline heard an irregular thumping sound outside. She was totally disoriented and first thought she was in her own home. Then she remembered and looked around Sheridan's living room. It was gray outside and the thumping continued. Toby sat with his ears sharply pointed.

She ran to the front door, thinking it was Sheridan kicking his boots outside. She turned on the light but the porch was empty. The thumping continued, but it was now clearly coming from the area of the barn.

She rushed into the kitchen and looked toward the barn. There stood the tall red horse. He was kicking the barn door in an effort to get in.

Caroline let out a cry and threw herself out of the

kitchen door with Toby in close pursuit. She shouted, Red, Red, where is Danny? Red, where is Danny? She looked all around the yard. The trucks and trailers of the rescue squad were still there. There was no sign of Sheridan.

She went to the great horse and threw her arm around his neck. Where is he, Red? The horse shook his head, as if to signal that he did not know. Then she looked down to see the horse favoring its left front foot, the one he had been swinging to hit the barn door. She opened the barn door as the light began to arrive. She led the horse inside and now saw that the saddle had slipped slightly sideways to the left. Sheridan's rifle was still in the scabbard. She struggled to loosen the cinch and slide the heavy saddle off. As she swung it to the ground she saw the scratches down the horse's left side and on its flank a couple of deep gashes.

She gasped and ran to the house as the horse nosed its feed bin. She raced toward the phone in the kitchen as it began to ring. *Thank God*, she thought. *He's calling to say he's alright. Or maybe someone else is.*

This is Steve Ramsey, the voice said. Is Dan Sheridan there? She could not bring herself to answer. Hello? This is Sheriff Ramsey. I'm calling for Mr. Sheridan.

Sheriff, she almost yelled, Thank God. This is Caroline Chandler. I've been here all night waiting for Daniel. Where is he?

He joined one of our search parties that went to rescue some kids up in the high country. He'll be back there soon. I got a walkie-talkie call from the group he was with and they're almost down to the Sheridan place.

Will he be with them? she pleaded. He's got to be with them.

There was a pause. Well, the sheriff said, now I'm a little mixed up. The team leader said they found the kids just as the storm came in. They got them packed up and started back. Apparently somewhere along the Silver Mesa Trail near Crystal Valley they got separated. The wind was up to thirty, forty miles an hour and making a hell of a howl and they couldn't hear themselves think. Dan waved them down the trail and they assumed he was right behind them. They got back to McClure Canyon when it cleared up enough for them to figure out he wasn't there. That's when they gave me a call reporting that they had the kids.

Where is he, Sheriff? she pleaded. He has to be somewhere with them.

Well, I'll be very honest with you, Ms. Chandler, I thought he had gotten out ahead of them. That he had beat them down and would be there at his house. That's why I called to make sure.

Sheriff, I'm frightened. I'm really frightened. I just woke up a couple of minutes ago and heard his horse outside. I let him in the barn and he's in bad shape. He is still winded and he's shivering cold. And his left side is all torn up.

My God, the Sheriff murmured. Alright, you wait right there. The horse vet is down at the bottom of Florida Road. I'll get him up there in fifteen minutes or less to look after the poor animal. I'll be in a squad car headed up the road ahead of him and should be there before he gets there. And about the time I get there my boys should be coming in. They may have figured something out.

Thank you, Sheriff, Caroline said. I need some help here. Please hurry.

She instinctively filled the large coffeepot and started

the fire under it. She got down on the floor and swept the border collie into her arms. Toby, Toby, she murmured. Then she began to weep.

After long minutes in which she felt her heart about to break apart, she remembered Red. Once again she ran out of the kitchen door with the dog running behind, went into the barn, and began to soothe the horse. Red, good boy, she kept saying. Red, good boy. She filled his large water bucket and he drank thirstily. She remembered where Sheridan kept the oats and put several shovelfuls into his grain trough.

She returned to the house and ran a bucket full of warm water and brought some worn towels. Once back in the barn, she began to wash the horse's wounds. He whinnied when she touched the particularly painful cuts, especially the deep ones on his flank. Once or twice he stamped his back foot in displeasure. But she continued on, constantly saying, Red, good boy. Where is he, Red? Where is Danny?

After a few minutes she heard a distant siren. It came closer and in another two minutes the sheriff screeched into the dirt driveway and threw on his brakes. The siren went silent, but the red and blue lights continued to flash.

The sheriff checked the house, then came to the barn. Any news, Ms. Chandler?

She shook her head and pointed to the horse's wounded side. He looked at the cuts closely and said, He's scraped against a canyon wall or a sharp outcropping. These cuts back here are pretty bad. The vet'll be here soon. He went to the horse's head and joined her in trying to calm the great creature down. That-a-boy, he said. That-a-boy. Good pony. Good pony.

Caroline stood apart now, nearby. She put her head in her hands and let her grief out. Where is he, Sheriff? Where is he? Please tell me he's alright.

Within minutes the vet arrived, came into the barn, and began to treat the horse. He examined the cuts and gashes. You've had quite a night, big fella, he said. Let's get some heavy disinfectant on those scrapes. He grabbed a handful of oats and put two big pills in them. He fed them to the horse from his palm. That-a-boy, he said. He searched his bag and came out with a bottle of colored liquid. He put on gloves and poured the liquid on sterile cloths. Then, carefully, he patted the medicine on the wounds. The horse whinnied and stamped his foot. The vet continued to soothe him, then said to the sheriff, He'll be okay. Go on inside.

Caroline led the sheriff inside and gave him a large mug of coffee. Outside, two Durango ambulances pulled up. Very quickly then Toby pushed open the screen door and went into the gate area and began to bark. That's them, the sheriff said. He put on his hat and they both went outside.

They'll tell us where he is, the sheriff told Caroline to comfort her.

The men came down the dirt road and into the barn area of the ranch. They let the three students down and then dismounted. The men and the horses looked exhausted. The sheriff directed the disheveled students to a waiting ambulance and they headed down Florida Road to the Durango hospital.

After the rescue crew had unsaddled their horses and put them in their trailers, Caroline brought them inside and gave them coffee. Having been in the saddle for hours, the

men milled around the kitchen trying to warm up. One of
the deputies said, It got pretty bad up there. We thought we
could get down last night, but several times you couldn't see
a thing, and we had to lay in under some pine groves until
the wind let up and we could see the trail with the flashlights.

One of the rangers looked at Caroline and said, Is Dan
around?

She shook her head and turned away as she started
to cry. The sheriff said, We thought he'd be coming down
with all of you. He didn't show up last night. Where did
you leave him?

Didn't leave him, Sheriff, the deputy said. We were
strung out along the trail when we started down. It was
black as pitch and blowin' like hell. He took the tail end
drag. By the time we had to lay up under the trees early
this morning, he wasn't there. Nor his horse. We figured
he knew a shorter way down or was lookin' for one. So
nobody thought much of it. He's pretty good at lookin' out
for himself.

One of the forest rangers said, I'm just surprised he's
not here waiting for us.

The sheriff said, It's not good, gentlemen. His horse
showed up a little while ago. He's pretty badly scratched up.

Caroline left the room.

Here's what I want you to do, the sheriff said. Get into
town, get something to eat, and rest up. I've put in a call to
the dispatcher. We've got another crew on its way up here
with fresh horses and we'll start them back up into the high
country as soon as they show up. I've also asked that heli-
copter to come back down from Grand Junction. And we've
got two light planes warming up at the Durango airport

right this minute. The dispatcher has given the pilots the exact coordinates of your trail and we'll just scour the territory until we find Mr. Sheridan.

57.

I'll check in on you from time to time, Ms. Chandler, the sheriff said. And you let me know when Dan shows up here. He looked her in the eye and said, He will show up here. I've known Daniel Sheridan all my life. There's no one in southwestern Colorado better able to get himself home than he is. Here's my numbers. Give me a call when he shows up.

Caroline said, He didn't have to go.

Yes, he did, the sheriff said. We could have lost some people up there. They all came back.

But he didn't, she said.

One by one the exhausted crew drove away. The sheriff followed. Twenty minutes later their replacements began to arrive. Caroline had made more coffee and handed it around to them in the yard as they unloaded the fresh horses and saddled them. They held huddled conversations around several maps, then organized themselves into two groups and headed back up the dirt road that formed the end of Florida Road and the beginning of McClure Canyon.

Caroline thought briefly about going upstairs to bed to wait. But she could not. He would be there. His scent would be there. She could not stand it. She kept the radio on for music and the possibility of some kind of announcement. In the news segment beginning each hour that slowly passed were reports of the ground-breaking ceremony that morning and excerpts from the speeches. Each time she had to turn away.

The vet had given her a salve for the horse's wounds, and each hour she found comfort in visiting the great creature in the barn and administering the ointment. When the horse whinnied in pain, she put her arm around his neck and talked into his ear. Good pony. Red's a good pony. Good boy, Red. Then, Where's Danny, Red?

Late morning she and Toby set out for the upper meadow of the Sheridan ranch. I'll see him coming down, she thought. I'll see him when he comes out of those trees. He's going to come out of those trees.

From time to time Toby whined softly. Each time it brought her own sighs and tears.

When she finally turned and came back down, she heard the telephone ringing in the house and raced to answer. It's Steve Ramsey, the sheriff said. Any news from up there?

No, she said. No news.

Our planes have come back for more fuel, he said. So far no sightings. They say the snow is still very heavy up there. That's good news because it makes locating someone easier. But it means it's also hard to get around. He didn't say "especially on foot," but she understood.

I'll stay in touch, he said. And you do the same.

She could only nod and thank him.

That evening the second search party returned. She dreaded to see them. Sheridan was not with them. She watched through binoculars as they emerged from the trees a quarter mile away. She counted the horses and riders. There were no double mounts.

At dusk she fed Toby. She herself could not eat. After he ate, Toby resumed his vigil at the kitchen door, standing and alert to any noise in the yard or barn, lying down and occasionally whining when all was silent. She took him with her to feed Red, administer the medicine, and settle him for the night.

At midnight she lay down on the leather sofa. Her last call from the sheriff had been two hours ago. She wept off and on until sleep came. Toby lay on the floor next to her.

Caroline stayed two more days at the Sheridan ranch. She could do nothing more. The vet promised to look in on Red from time to time and Harv Waldron's son called to say he would feed the horse and dog and look after the place until Dan Sheridan returned.

Caroline drove through the battered gate, then closed it, and drove down Florida Road toward home. She held the carved figure of the Indian woman tightly in one hand as she drove.

58.

On the outskirts of Ignacio on the Southern Ute reservation, Two Hawks, the ancient holy man, emerged onto his porch as the first rays of the sun broke the horizon.

He faced the east and raised his arms and began to pray. He continued his prayer as he turned to the south, then to the west, and finally to the north. He prayed to the spirit of the four seasons and the four compass points. He prayed for all the creatures and for all the Indian people. He prayed for the white men in Durango and everywhere else.

Then, in the language of the Ute people, he prayed this prayer:

Be with our friend Daniel Sheridan, Great Spirit.

He is a warrior with a great heart.

He has the cougar's soul.

He will find us when it is his time.

The End

Afterword

For a number of years it has been my honor to be published by Fulcrum Publishing of Golden, Colorado, a publisher with roots in the West and a deep concern for western history, progressive public policy, protection of nature and Her creatures, and, most of all, quality books. To its owners and officers Robert Baron and Sam Scinta I owe a deep debt of gratitude, especially for appreciating why the story of *Durango* deserves to be told.

This story brings one of Sophocles' lesser-known plays, *Philoctetes*, into the late twentieth century. For those interested in parallels, as the epigraph suggests, the best rendering of *Philoctetes* in recent times is Seamus Heaney's *The Cure at Troy*. Instead of the Trojan War, though, this story involves a real-life water conflict in southwestern Colorado.

Water wars, great and small, form a kind of history of the American West. Few, at least in recent times, have involved bloodshed. But I have it on knowledgeable authority that the tense conflict represented by the Animas–La Plata water project central to this story is, if anything, understated.

It is one thing to write a story based on genuine history. It is even more complex to write that story when you yourself played a small role in it. It is as true to history as I could make it, with the considerable help of Mr. Tom

Shipps and Professor Duane Smith. Mr. Shipps was the law partner of the late Sammy Maynes (Sam Maynard). And Professor Smith (Duane Smithson) is the dean of Colorado historians and the acknowledged expert on southwestern Colorado history. They both made invaluable contributions to this story, especially having to do with the history of the region and the laws surrounding the Animas–La Plata water and the Southern Ute tribal resources.

A few others in the story are based on real people past and present. Frances Farnsworth, together with the Southern Ute holy man Two Hawks, form the moral compass and the community conscience of the story. Frances is very loosely based on the late Morley Ballantine, who, with her husband, Arthur, owned and published the *Durango Herald* during much of the period of this narration.

There is no actual Daniel Sheridan or Caroline Chandler, though people like them surely exist somewhere, possibly even in Durango.

This is a story of the modern West, with roots in the history of the West's first Americans and those of us who overwhelmed them, and in western resources, particularly its water.

I choose to believe the gracious Southern Ute tribal chairman Leonard Burch and his legendary Durango lawyer Sammy Maynes are somewhere up in the Weminuche, catching fish, telling stories, drinking whiskey, and laughing.

I hope to join them there someday.

Gary Hart
Kittredge, Colorado